REBELLIOUS ROCKSTAR

THE BURNT CLOVERS

GINA AZZI

Rebellious Rockstar

Copyright © 2023 by Gina Azzi

No part of this publication may be reproduced, distributed, or transmitted in any form or by any means, including photocopying, recording, or other electronic or mechanical methods, without the prior written permission of the publisher, except in the case of brief quotations embodied in critical reviews and certain other noncommercial uses permitted by copyright law.

This is a work of fiction. Names, characters, businesses, places, events, locales, and incidents are either the products of the author's imagination or used in a fictitious manner. Any resemblance to actual persons, living or dead, or actual events is purely coincidental.

To all the epic loves that just won't quit.

ONE
ALLEGRA

The taxi comes to a stop in front of the brownstone. Four years ago, it was a disheveled property no one looked at twice. Now, it's an iconic piece of history.

Anticipation rolls down my spine and I arch my back to shake it off.

I roll my shoulders back and exhale. I've got this. Deep down, I know this is where I'm meant to be. It's one step closer to figuring out my future; it's the page turn that begins my next chapter.

I spent the bus ride from Los Angeles to Boston mentally mapping out my next steps. I confirmed informational interviews with NGOs and RSVP'd yes to workshops hosted by advocacy groups around the city.

I'm committed to strengthening my relationship with my brother Levi. Since I left for UCLA, our once unshakeable bond has loosened and frayed. Now, one sharp tug could snap it completely.

Everything I desire for my future is right here in Boston, only an hour train ride from the hometown I was once desperate to escape. I roll my lips together to keep from smiling at the irony.

Yes, I'm back in town the way my parents predicted. But I'm not cowering, with slumped shoulders and my tail between my legs. So, it's not exactly as they hoped.

Instead, I'm rocking skintight leather leggings and a crop top. When I arrived at the terminal this morning, I perfected my makeup, carefully creating that natural, dewy, "glowing-from-the-inside" look and using half a can of dry shampoo to hide the greasiness of my hair.

A bus ride across the country provided ample time to hype me up for my future. It also allowed uninterrupted hours to obsess over what it will be like to see Derek Reiner, rebellious rockstar and international heartthrob, for the first time in four years. Since the night he gave me my first kiss. I bite my bottom lip, recalling the way his mouth felt moving over mine.

Reign, as he's known to his fans, gave me my first kiss on my seventeenth birthday. Back then, he was just Derek. Who will he be to me now?

A shiver races up my spine. Hope is a dangerous emotion. Volatile and fickle yet carefully concealed as conviction.

"You want me to circle the block?" the cab driver asks, not unkindly. I glance at him. He shrugs. "It'll cost you. Traffic's picking up."

It's time to find out what the future holds. This is why I took a leave of absence from UCLA; this is why I'm here.

"No, I'm good," I say, tapping my debit card against the machine to settle the cab fare. My stomach tightens as I mentally calculate how much money is left in my checking account. Since my brother Levi, Derek's bandmate, doesn't know I'm coming and Mom and Dad have stopped sending me an allowance when they learned I started skipping church, my funds are low. I hope one of those informational interviews segues into a paid summer internship.

"Take care," the cabbie remarks, trying to hurry me along.

"Right. You too." I slip from the back seat. I move to the back of the car as he pops the trunk. Heaving out my suitcase, I offer a little wave but he's already pulling back onto the road.

I pause in front of the brownstone, look up at the charming facade, and smile. Even though four millionaires, rock gods, veritable celebrities live inside, they haven't changed the appearance of their humble beginnings. Instead, their home away from home, their band headquarters, blends in with the rest of the street.

Squaring my shoulders, I take a deep breath and ascend the steps. Dropping my suitcase, I knock on the door. I wipe my hands down the length of my black leggings. My sandal taps against the ground.

Levi is going to be pissed. That's okay; I've been angry with him for the better part of the past year.

But what will Derek think? Will he remember me? Will he—

"Yeah?" a guy answers, his head turned away when he pulls open the door.

I try to clear my throat but am frozen to the spot. I drink in the back of his head, note the tattoos that crawl over his knuckles, wrap around his wrist, as he grips the doorframe.

He swings around, his eyes collide with mine, and surprise—unfiltered and genuine—washes over Derek Reiner's face. "Stellina?" His voice is a hushed whisper, his eyes a kaleidoscope of emotions. He blinks and they're gone, save for uncertainty.

Stellina. It moves through my body like an electric current. My hope soars.

Little star.

It's what he called me the night of my birthday. He kissed me softly and told me that I was too big for my small town in Massachusetts. That I'd already outgrown it.

You're the most beautiful, captivating, mesmerizing woman here.

None of those girls hold a fucking candle to a little star like you.

His words from that night, so long ago, roll through my mind like he just said them. Like no time has passed.

His eyes narrow, his jaw tightens.

But it's been four years.

I smile, feign a hell of a lot more casual than I feel. Breathe. "Hey, Derek. Long time no see."

"Who's at the door?" I recognize my brother's voice in the background. "Please tell me you ordered food. I'm fucking starving and we need to hit the studio."

Derek's eyes are still glued to mine. Intense and...angry. "What are you doing here?"

I force myself to stand straighter. The space between my shoulder blades pinches and I lift my chin. Derek's eyes narrow. They drop to my chest for a heartbeat and narrow even more before snapping back up.

I fight the urge to laugh.

There's nothing I'd like more than for Reign to check me out. Hard.

But that's not *exactly* what I'm here for. At least, not yet.

"Is Levi home?" I ask, even though I know he is.

"He doesn't know you're coming," Derek deduces.

"I messaged him but—" Levi appears behind Derek, and I halt my explanation.

Concern washes over my brother's face. "A." He smacks Derek's hand off the doorframe and steps out onto the stoop. "What're you doing here?" He pulls me into a hug. "Are you okay? Mom and Dad?" At the hint of fear in his tone, I know he still worries for our parents, still loves them in his own way. I also realize he hasn't spoken with them in far too long if he's asking me—the student who *should* be in California—that question.

"They're fine," I reply, pulling back. I try to smile but it wobbles as an old wound, a dull ache, blooms at the base of my throat. Levi doesn't know I withdrew from college. Did he read any of my messages? Listen to my voice notes? Does he care? "I tried getting in touch with you."

A sheepish expression slips over his face, and he grips the back of his neck. "Yeah, sorry, A. Been busy."

In the doorframe, Derek crosses his arms over his chest and leans against the doorjamb. He glares at my brother's profile.

"You need something? Money?" Levi asks, shuffling from one foot to the other. He's antsy, on edge. Instead of welcoming me into his home, he's trying to rush me off his front porch.

Hurt slams into me, full-on, like a sucker punch. Levi's actions, his disregard, pull the air from my lungs, and I fight the urge to fold in on myself. To disappear. My hand lifts to my chest, pressing there, as I stare at my brother, unable to speak.

At Levi's question, Derek's eyes jump to mine. A muscle in his jaw tics.

Embarrassment burns through me, causing my cheeks to blaze. I wish Derek would give me a moment alone with my brother. Trying to explain why I'm here, what I'm doing, under his watchful gaze is unsettling.

For a heartbeat, I feel like a bumbling seventeen-year-old again, insecure, and never been kissed. I grip the handle of my suitcase and shuffle back half a step. Fight or flight. Right now, I want to bolt as fast as my feet will take me.

It's as if Derek knows my thoughts. At least, he understands more than my brother. Because he hitches forward, leaning toward my frame, as if pulled by an invisible thread. His eyes lock on mine. Pierce and hold. Entrance and captivate.

And in his gaze, I find the strength to shake off my nerves. To hold fast to my resolve.

I know why I'm here. I know what I want. And part of that is a relationship with my brother, even if it takes time to cultivate. Even if I need to put in more effort.

Hell, I've got the entire summer.

I take a deep breath and mentally flip through options.

If Levi won't welcome me with open arms, I'll try a different tactic. I'll regroup entirely and form a new strategy. I won't stand on his porch and embarrass myself in front of him. In front of Derek.

I narrow my eyes and flip my chin at Levi. "Forget it. I'm out." I tug my suitcase closer and turn but the handle is yanked from my grasp.

When I spin around, Derek is glowering. "Get inside," he demands, turning away from the stoop and taking my suitcase with him.

I hesitate, but Levi wraps an arm around my shoulder and directs me into the brownstone. Is he inviting me inside because it's his brotherly duty? Because he cares? Or because Reign told him to?

I hate that Option C seems to be the correct answer.

"What's going on, A?" My brother tries again but I hear the frustration in his tone.

Is he annoyed that he doesn't know what's going on? Or is he annoyed that I'm here, interrupting his life, and invading his space?

My embarrassment flirts with anger and marries hurt.

"I took a leave of absence. From UCLA," I announce once we're in the living room.

No one moves to sit, and we stand around in an awkward huddle, with Derek still gripping my suitcase like a hostage and me staying closest to the front door.

"What?" My brother's eyes widen. "Why the hell did you do that?"

"Did something happen?" Derek asks, his expression morphing from anger to concern in a heartbeat. "Someone hurt you?"

His thought process is another echo from the past. When he found me crying on the roof of a barn and thought my crush hurt me, pressured me, when in reality, Grant rejected me for my friend Cynthia. To make me feel better, Derek kissed me, gifting me the best birthday gift.

"No," I say quickly. "I'm taking the summer to sort out my future and plan my next steps."

"What's there to sort out?" Derek snaps. "You go to school, graduate, and get a job." He points at me. "You're not supposed to be here."

Levi heaves out a sigh. "Do Mom and Dad know?"

"That I took a leave of absence or that I'm here?" I ask, ignoring the hurt that's taken root in my stomach at Derek's words.

"Either. Both." Levi crosses his arms over his chest, giving me the big brother routine.

I roll my eyes. "Yes, they know I'm taking a break. No, they don't know I'm here."

"You need to go home," Levi commands. He rakes his fingers through his hair, looking down as if I'm a problem he needs to deal with. As if my showing up to surprise him, to spend time with him, to figure out my future, is the biggest inconvenience of his life.

I arch an eyebrow. Lean forward to note the open concept living room that leads into the kitchen. I glance at the butcher block kitchen island and neat row of barstools.

Nah, Levi's doing just fine. My presence shouldn't rattle him, and I refuse to let it.

"You're going to make shit between me and Mom and Dad even worse," my brother mutters. "It's bad enough you dropped out—"

"Took a leave of absence," I correct.

"But you came here?" Levi's eyes find mine. "Don't burn your bridge home to Mom and Dad's for me, A. I'm not worth it."

I clasp my hands behind my back, pinching the skin at the base of my wrist to keep my composure. How did Levi make this about him? What happened to my big brother? The one who used to protect me and care about my feelings? The one who loved me unconditionally?

I squint at this new version and hardly recognize him.

I heave out an exhale. If anyone is shouldering a boulder of disappointment in this room, it's me. I left college to figure out my future, to define what I want out of life. I thought I'd find a safe space at my brother's but if that's not the case, I'll figure it out on my own.

"Fine," I say, my voice more composed than I feel. I reach forward and jerk the suitcase handle out of Derek's grasp. "I'll head to Cynthia's. She's not too far—"

"Your friend that hooked up with the guy you liked?" Derek asks incredulously.

Levi's eyes swing to him, confusion momentarily masking his feelings of frustration.

Even though my stomach twists at Derek's reminder, my heart rate accelerates that he remembers. He can recall that night as quickly as I can. That must count for something, right?

Sure, Cynthia and I have a complicated relationship. In the past, I felt inferior to her, and she relished feeling superior to me. At best, we're frenemies. Except I'm too composed to indulge in the enemy tactics she dabbles in—like hooking up with your friend's crush at her birthday party.

But we have history. It dates to the second grade, and I know for a fact that she wouldn't turn me away or question my decisions the way Levi and Derek are.

"Cynthia's a mess," Levi mutters. "Last time I saw her, guys were lining up to take body shots off her over at Taps. It's her new thing."

Derek mutters a string of profanities that sounds like, "that stupid fucking sports bar where the Hawks and puck bunnies hang out."

I shrug. "I'll still be welcomed there." I move toward the door, my suitcase in tow.

I begin to pull it open when a strong hand plants in the center, right over my head, slamming it closed. I whirl around and inhale sharply as my chest skims across Derek's abdomen.

He glares down at me, his whiskey eyes tumultuous. His jaw is clenched, a muscle popping.

I drag in a breath, letting his scent—fresh soap and mint—wash over me.

I lift my eyebrows in a silent question. In a challenge. *Should I leave?*

"No," he replies to my non-verbal thought. "Absolutely not," he tacks on, dropping his hand to look at my brother. "If St—Allegra stays in Boston, she stays right fucking here. Where we can keep an eye on her."

Levi levels him with a look, thrown by Derek's decision. He's silent for a long moment and it strikes me that he doesn't question Derek the way he does me. His gaze lands on my face. "You'll call Mom and Dad and tell them the truth? Last thing I need is them thinking I've corrupted you, brought you over to the dark side."

I nod. "I'll tell them."

"Fine," he mutters. Then, he pulls in an inhale and his expression softens. He opens his arms and holds them out, waiting for me.

I cock my head and stare at him for a long moment, letting him feel the same rejection he just tossed my way.

After several uncomfortable seconds, he snorts. "Come on, A. Give me a fucking hug."

Rolling my eyes, I step into his arms and give him a tight squeeze. Nostalgia rolls through me, and I remember our simple, sweet childhood. I let him hold me for an extra beat because now that I'm here, it feels nice. Safe.

"Thanks, Levi," I murmur into the cotton of his T-shirt. I should probably be thanking Derek.

Levi chuckles, the vibration of his laughter pulsing against my cheek. "Don't thank me yet, A. You have no clue what you're in for."

TWO
DEREK

I can't tear my eyes away from her.

Jesus. Why the hell is she here complicating shit?

And who wears leather leggings in the summer anyway?

She moves up onto her tippy toes as Levi hugs her and the curve of her ass, stretching the leather fabric, taunts me. Tempts me.

She was beautiful at seventeen but now, she's a siren, calling to all the fucked-up parts of me she has no business mixing with.

Levi releases her and I tear my eyes away before my bandmate—my best friend—catches me ogling his baby sister. I know for a fact the way I'm checking Allegra out isn't big brotherly. Nope, there's nothing platonic about the way my hands want to roam her curves or how I can still taste her sweet kiss when I've hooked up with countless—nameless—women since her.

We didn't even hook up. We kissed. It was so PG I shouldn't remember it. It shouldn't register. The fact that it does unnerves me. Allegra unnerves me.

I huff out a breath. I don't want her here, in my space, in my city, under my goddamn roof all summer.

But the thought of her hanging with Cynthia and tangling up in her bullshit bugs me even more.

Levi slugs an arm around Allegra's shoulder. "Come on. You can bunk with Mav."

I start at the stupid suggestion. Is Levi dense? He's gonna put his baby sister in the same room as our drummer? Maverick Tate isn't anything like his big brother, our bass player, Jameson.

While Jameson is locked down, banging the same woman since high school, Mav is a pranking, easygoing, life-of-the-party kinda dude who pulls women in with his blue eyes and baby face and leaves them crying the next morning when he promises *not* to call.

I start toward Levi. "Levi, I think—"

My friend swings his gaze toward mine. His eyes narrow and his jawline tightens, and I note that my interfering in his family shit with his sister just ended. As much as I don't like it, I respect it. I hold my hands up in surrender. "I'll bring up Allegra's suitcase."

"You do that," Levi bites out.

Damn. We'll have words later. He doesn't want his sister here any more than I do. But while I need her gone so I don't do something I'll regret, like jeopardize the stability of the band, he doesn't want her here because it makes his shit with his parents more complicated.

And their relationship is a mindfuck on heroin.

I trail after them, taking Allegra's suitcase with me. It's lighter than I thought it would be. Did she leave her belongings in California? Is this all she has? Both thoughts bother me, and I shake them off.

"You sure about this?" Levi asks.

"Absolutely," Allegra replies. She's decisive. It's a far cry from the girl I met four years ago and yet, I can't tamp down the flicker of pride that sparks in my chest.

Good for her.

"What are you going to do all summer?" Levi adds like he had his whole fucking life sorted at twenty-one-years-old.

"I'll figure it out," she responds cryptically.

I duck my head to hide my smile. I like that she's knocking her brother down a few pegs. He needs it.

Allegra catches my grin and her eyes spark. There's a playful gleam that wasn't there the night I met her. But underneath, that sweet softness, that genuine authenticity, flares. It sobers me. Transports me back in time.

To the night of her seventeenth birthday and that stupid bonfire by a barn in the middle of fucking nowhere in her small town. To the way she looked after some golden boy baseball player with stars in her eyes. To her fallen expression and slumped shoulders when she admitted she'd never been kissed.

Levi flips on the light to Mav and Jameson's room. "I'll tell Mav to clean his shit up," he offers, glancing around the mess. Swearing, Levi bends and pockets a red thong Mav's last conquest left behind as a souvenir.

Allegra wraps one hand around the ladder to the top bunk. "Where's Jameson?"

"Pussy whipped," I mutter.

Allegra snorts.

Levi sighs. Grips the back of his neck. "He pretty much lives with his girlfriend."

"Amelia," Allegra supplies.

"Yeah, her." Levi nods. "She comes around sometimes..."

Allegra glances between Levi and me, but neither of us

offers the information we're thinking. Amelia's a bitch, and Jameson should drop her ass. The last time she stepped out on Jameson, she gutted him.

I drop the suitcase with a thud, garnering both Rousell siblings' attention.

"If you're gonna stay, we have rules," I spit out.

Levi raises his eyebrows. "Really? What are they?"

I glare at him. He smirks.

I point at Allegra. "No men."

Her eyes widen. "Excuse me?"

Levi scowls. "Come on, man. A just got here. She's not dating any—"

"No boyfriends. No random hook-ups," I clarify. "We don't need any strangers knowing our address."

Allegra snickers. "The red thong wearer is in the circle of trust?"

I almost grin at her sarcasm but hold back. If she thinks she can get her way with that smart mouth and those hooded, bedroom eyes, I'm fucked. Well, more fucked than I already am.

Levi shakes his head, stares at his sister in disbelief. "Allegra doesn't hook up wi—"

"How do you know?" she challenges him, her eyes sparking. Her gaze darts between the two of us. "I wouldn't bring a man back here out of respect for you. For your headquarters or whatever the hell you call this place."

Levi winces when she says *hell* and I realize how he still sees Allegra. The same way his parents do—pristine, naïve, and fragile. A little girl.

The woman standing before me is none of those things and while I love witnessing her ferocity, I don't like her attitude on the topic of men.

"Good," I state.

She grins. "Obviously, I'd go back to his place."

Levi's mouth drops open in shock. I swear.

Before either of us can respond, little Ms.-Fragile-My-Ass points to the bedroom door. "If you'll give me some privacy, I'd like to shower and change. It's been a long bus ride."

"You took a fucking bus here?" I roar.

"From LA?" Levi looks truly bewildered. And alarmed.

Jesus, mate, do you know nothing about your sister?

Allegra crosses her arms. A patch of red—anger, embarrassment, maybe both—crawls up her chest, colors the base of her throat, flames into her cheeks.

Footsteps pound the stairs, and we all turn as Maverick crashes into the room. He pulls up short when he spots his new roommate. His eyes widen, trail down her body slowly, and a smile spreads across his expression.

I punch him in the shoulder. Hard enough to make him wince.

"What the fuck, Reign?" He grips his arm.

"This is Allegra. *Levi's sister*," I spit out.

Levi scrubs a hand down his face. "I messaged you, Mav. Is it cool if she bunks with you for—"

"Hi." Allegra steps forward, holding out a hand. "I'm Allegra Rousell. If it's not too much trouble, would it be cool to room together for the summer? I'm...in between life plans."

Levi watches his sister carefully. As if he's just noticing that she grew up into a gorgeous and capable woman.

Mav shakes her hand and grins at her. "Abso-fucking-lutely. More than cool, Allegra Rousell. These in-between life plans...like, rehab?"

Levi swears.

Allegra laughs.

And I freeze. The sound of her laughter is a punch to the gut. It's…beautiful. And I hate it because at the appreciation that flickers in Mav's eyes, I know he hears it too.

Her sincerity. Her candor.

I don't want him to have those pieces of her. I don't want anyone, not even me, to have them.

"Nah. Like, college," she supplies.

"Got it." He drops her hand. "I'll clear some closet space for you. My brother is hardly around so I took over. But it'll be cool to have a roomie again. We can stay up late, share secrets." He winks.

"Braid each other's hair?" she deadpans.

Levi snorts.

Mav's smile grows. "I already like you, Allegra Rousell."

"Stop saying her full name," I snap.

Mav rolls his eyes without glancing in my direction. He slugs an arm around Allegra's shoulders. "We gotta head to the studio in a few. Wanna come? We'll grab a bite afterwards."

Allegra smiles at him. Her face wide open, her dark eyes warm like cocoa, her expression playful. She's fierce like a thunderbolt. Heartfelt like sunshine.

She's confusing as fuck, and as much as I want to turn around and walk away, a larger part of me wants to stand here, all day, and listen to her talk. Study her movements. Learn what the hell caused her to take a bus across the country and knock on our front door.

"Sure," she agrees. She tips her head toward the door. "Do I have time for a quick shower? My bus ride was brutal."

Mav wrinkles his nose. "Where'd you come from?"

"LA," she offers, unzipping her suitcase and gathering a few items.

"Damn," Mav mutters. "I once took a bus from Boston to Houston, and I thought that sucked."

"So, you understand my need for a hot shower?" Allegra stands, holding a bundle of clean clothes against her chest.

"More than these two." Mav hooks his thumb toward Levi and me. He drops his voice to a conspiratorial whisper. "They only fly business class."

Allegra laughs again as Mav leads her to the bathroom in the hallway.

My jaw tics.

Levi looks lost.

I dig the heels of my hands into my eyes. A tension headache is coming on.

It's gonna be a long, insufferable summer.

THREE
ALLEGRA

Watching the band collaborate at the studio is different than I expected. Firstly, it's not nearly as glamorous as I thought it'd be. While the studio equipment is top notch, there isn't free-flowing champagne and fashion models hanging around.

Clearly, all my knowledge about the music industry is what I've gleaned from television shows and movies. Considering my brother is a member of The Burnt Clovers, the realization saddens me. How did Levi and I grow so far apart in such a short number of years? How do I know nothing about his life, save for the parts that piss off Mom and Dad, and he knows nothing of mine, at all?

As the band plays, my sadness is replaced with excitement. Sitting in on their session, witnessing the energy that syncs between them is incredible. All four members are so different in terms of looks and personalities but in the booth together, they seamlessly blend, becoming something greater than their individual traits.

The collaborative spirit of their session, the way they

build off each other's ideas, always willing to try something new, is inspiring.

I've never heard these songs, and I realize the band is recording a new album. While they're still fiddling with the lyrics and chords, taking breaks to try changes and make notes, they're creating a masterpiece. A series of hits that will play on an endless loop on radio stations across the country in the coming months.

A few songs in and I'm completely, wholeheartedly captured by Derek. The sound of his voice, raspy and sultry, moves over my skin like a cool breeze. The column of his neck, the veins that ripple in his forearms, the slight shadow that coats the underside of his jaw, is visceral and sexy. He pours himself into his music, giving a glimmer of the man that lives beneath the phenomenon, concealed by a strong jaw and a blasé attitude.

My hands fist in my lap, my throat too dry to swallow. But I don't clear it; I barely blink. I can't tear my eyes from Derek Reiner if my sanity depends on it. And right now, it probably does.

The night he kissed me explodes in my mind. The cold night air, the callouses on his fingertips, the heat of his mouth, firm and fathomless against mine. I shiver.

I've recounted that night, that moment, for years. It still affects me. Derek, larger-than-life and famous, still belongs to me in some small way that most would dismiss as insignificant. To me, it's a defining moment of my life.

As Derek croons into the microphone, his eyes closed, his tatted knuckles flexing on the mic, I come back to the moment. To the now. His eyes open and collide with mine.

Hold. Pierce. Know.

So dark they're nearly black, glinting with swirling emotions I don't understand, he sings *to me*. At least, it feels that way. Time stops, the energy around me crackles to life, the air particles between Derek and me shrinking and expanding until I'm not sure if I'm in the past or present, in reality or a dream.

"You vanished like daybreak,
Lost stars and forgotten night.
You haunt me like a shadow,
Clingy and relentless.
You haunt me like her."

He sings the chorus, the skull on the back of his hand shifting as he regrips the microphone. The navy nail polish on his right fingernails dances as he taps a beat along his thigh.

"You haunt me like her."

The song ends. I work a desperate swallow. Swipe my clammy palms along my shorts. Derek blinks. Our connection severs.

My mind reels and I try to regulate my breathing. Who haunts him? Who is the woman like her? And who the hell is the "her" in the song? Did he write this? One of the other guys? A random songwriter?

I shake my head. It doesn't matter. It doesn't mean anything.

My heart kicks behind my breastplate, calling me out.

Because it does mean something. To me, it means more than it should.

"Nice work, guys," the sound engineer says.

The producer claps his hands as the guys file out of the booth. My brother smiles at me. Mav tosses an arm over my shoulders.

"What'd you think?" Mav asks.

"You guys are...incredible," I admit, my gaze flickering to Derek.

He doesn't glance in my direction. Doesn't acknowledge my praise.

"Hey. I'm Jameson." A guy with a slight resemblance to Mav flips his chin at me.

I lift my hand in a wave. "Allegra. Levi's sister."

Jameson smirks. "Heard you're bunking with my brother."

Mav hugs me closer. I smile. "Yep."

Jameson's smirk grows. "Keep him in line, yeah?"

"I'll do my best," I promise.

Mav and Jameson laugh.

Their producer, Sam, goes over a few things with them. Then, Levi claps his hands. "Ready to eat?"

"Let's head to the pub," Mav agrees.

Jameson hangs his head. "Uh, I—"

"Gotta get home to the wifey?" Derek supplies, his eyes narrowed.

Jameson shrugs. "You know how it is."

Levi snorts. "Not really, man." He clasps hands with Jameson, and they do some bro handshake. "But you do you."

"Take care. Good meeting you," Jameson says to me.

"You too," I say as he slips out of the studio.

"Your brother's gotta cut Amelia loose," Derek comments to Mav.

Mav doesn't reply but his arm around my shoulders tightens.

Derek shrugs, as if shaking off the negative energy he just brought into the room, into the band dynamics. "Let's go."

I follow after the guys, slip into the back of a black Escalade, and take a moment to myself as we drive to a pub. Large trees, full of greenery and summer, mix with cobblestone streets as Boston slips past outside my window.

In the background, the guys talk, dissecting their studio time.

From snippets of their conversation, I glean that they're recording a new album this summer and are still working out the lyrics for three of the songs. Derek seems the most frustrated by their setbacks, with Mav and Levi shrugging it off.

"Just wanna go out and enjoy summer," Levi admits.

I bite the inside of my cheek to stop my retort.

Will Levi and I grow closer if we're in the same place, or has too much time passed? Are we too different now to connect on the things we used to have in common, namely, our family?

I blow out a sigh. I have a call later tonight with a woman, Genevieve Yaeger, who runs the Harrison Foundation and does a lot of work with women's shelters, centering on female education and empowerment, in Boston. My roommate Mckenna hooked me up with her contact and I'm excited to speak with her and get involved with the programs her foundation runs.

Will I discover the type of work I want to commit my career to? Will any of them lead to full-time employment? Was taking a leave of absence from UCLA the right decision?

Questions circle my mind in rapid succession. Too quickly to search for answers. Too quickly to offer reassurances.

I feel his gaze on my cheek. The weight of his stare pulls me from my thoughts and a hyperawareness of my surroundings grows. The fabric of my denim shorts and the way they ride up when I sit, exposing my tanned thighs.

The ends of my hair that brush against my shoulders when I tilt my neck. I press my palms together to halt my expanding nerves.

"You're overthinking it," he murmurs.

I turn toward him, my eyes snapping to his. They're guarded but I note the hint of frustration that curls his upper lip.

"Overthinking what?" I ask.

Derek shrugs, stretching out his legs so the denim of his jeans skims along my bare calf. It's rough against my smooth skin. "Everything."

I smirk. "You don't know what I'm thinking about."

He bites his bottom lip, the indent of his top teeth grazing against his full lip. His eyelids lower to half mast, hooded and hot. "Want me to guess?"

I press my hands tighter, try to control the hitch in my breathing. I squirm under his gaze, and he grins.

"That's what I thought," he says causally, his expression blank and blasé once more.

I frown, not understanding what transpired between us. What does he want me to say? What does he mean? His speaking in riddles is frustrating but so are his hot and cold moods. Already, he's giving me whiplash.

I don't like this feeling. I relish being in control of my thoughts and emotions. Of my interactions with guys.

Before I can press him for a real answer, for some understanding at what game he's playing at, the SUV rolls to a stop in a back alley. The four of us exit the Escalade and are greeted by a guy at the back entrance.

"What's good, Duke?" Levi exchanges a backslap with the older man.

"Good to see you, boys. Come on in." Duke props the door wider.

I follow the guys through a dimly lit corridor and emerge in the back of a pub. Duke points to a corner booth and we slip inside.

"Been coming here for years," Levi explains.

"Duke's always been good to us," Mav tacks on.

"Even lent us money when we were starting out," Levi adds, passing me a menu.

A muscle pops in Derek's jaw and his fingers, gripping the underside of the table, tighten. They're small movements, almost imperceptible. But I'm so in tune to him, I catch them. I just don't know what they mean.

A breathless server appears at the end of our table. She giggles, tucks a strand of hair behind her ear, and looks over her shoulder. It's then that I notice that a group of women have repositioned themselves at the end of the bar closest to our booth.

I fight the urge to laugh. Do these women think Levi or Mav or Derek are just going to walk over and buy them a drink? I frown and glance at my brother. He's craning his neck to check them out. Gah, is that how this works?

If so, it's too…desperate. So pointless.

There's no chase. No conversation. No thrill or anticipation.

"The redhead is hot," Levi mutters.

The server blushes and drops her eyes to her notepad.

Internally, I groan. Of course Levi commented.

Derek sighs. "We'll take a pitcher of whatever IPA you have on tap." He glances at me. "You drink beer? Or are you too prissy to—"

"A doesn't really drink," Levi cuts in.

"Beer's fine." I arch an eyebrow at my brother.

Surprise ripples over his expression but he backs down.

"Let's get the nachos, some yam fries, wings, two pounds—" Mav starts to rattle off appetizers.

The guys all order burgers but I opt for mac and cheese. Once our server is gone, all three guys swivel to stare at the women sitting at the bar.

The women glance in our direction shamelessly. They shift on their barstools, arch their backs, and one even daringly sucks on the end of a cherry.

I watch, a little grossed out, as Levi brazenly enjoys the attention. His eyes bounce from one woman to the next. I can see his mind turning, mentally calculating their assets, adding and subtracting which combination of parts will best satisfy him tonight.

It's repulsive.

Has he always been like this around women? Did he used to hide it around me better? Or has his newfound fame erased his common decency? My disappointment in Levi flares.

As a second woman leans over to lick the cherry her friend sucked on, I laugh.

"This is really something," I comment, leaning back in my chair to watch the show these women are putting on. "You should've ordered popcorn," I tell Mav.

He chuckles.

Levi glares at me. Then, he swears and slips from the booth. He glances at Derek. "You gonna wingman me or what?"

Derek gives me a side look before grinning and following my brother to the bar.

"Don't feel obligated to sit here and babysit me," I tell Mav. "I'm a big girl."

My new roommate/friend's eyes dart to the bar before sliding back to me. "You sure? Just real quick; there's a girl I recognize. And this pub is kind of like our second home. No one bothers us here, but everyone knows this is where we chill."

I gesture toward the bar. "Have at it."

Mav leaves too and I'm left alone, watching as women practically fall at the feet of the band members. Is it always like this? Is that why Jameson ditched hanging to go home to his girlfriend? I look around the nondescript, worn-in pub. Can Levi and the guys go anywhere anymore? Or is this—the women, the attention, the alluring temptation—their new normal?

Within minutes, a leggy brunette has a palm planted on Derek's abs. She laughs at something he says which is mind-boggling because I don't think he possesses a sense of humor. I stare at them, practically squinting to clock every second of their exchange. Derek places his hand on top of hers, trapping it against his hard body.

The server drops off the pitcher and glasses.

I pour myself a beer. Take two large gulps.

The brunette nuzzles closer, and Derek lets her. As he says something to Levi over her shoulder, she kisses up his neck, nibbling on the underside of his jaw. He barely reacts, other than to stretch his neck and give her more room to play.

A flare of pain shoots through me. What did I think was going to happen? There's nothing between me and Derek. There never was. The fantasies I've harbored all these years were nothing more than girlish ruminations.

The server appears again with nachos and yam fries. She doesn't spare me a second glance.

Derek's eyes find mine as the brunette wraps her arms around him, palming his ass and kissing the corner of his mouth. He smirks. His eyes glint with a challenge.

Ugh. I look away, blinking back the irrational tears mixed with anger that prick the corners of my eyes. This is stupid. I'm not going to sit here, all alone, and let the guys have all the fun.

I stuff a nacho in my mouth before swiping up my beer and relocating to the other side of the bar. The side with clusters of men, watching a European soccer match on a television screen over the bar.

I can get behind a soccer game. Especially a match between Madrid and Barcelona. Taking an empty barstool, I sip my beer. "Uff, El Clásico, huh?"

The guy beside me turns. His lip is curled but when he sees me, he chuckles. "It's gonna be intense." He leans casually against the ledge of the bar. And he's hot. Blond hair, longer on top. Blue eyes. A dimple in his right cheek.

"Always," I agree. The rivalry between Barcelona and Real Madrid dates back over one-hundred-twenty years.

"Who are you rooting for?" he asks, a glint to his eyes.

I scoff. "Real Madrid. Of course."

He groans and places a hand over his chest. "You're breaking my heart."

I arch an eyebrow. "That's all it took?"

Two of his friends laugh, chiming in to rib him. They move closer, forming a little huddle around my barstool. We talk smack and joke around throughout the first period.

Barcelona scores and a cheer rings out, even as I drop my face into my hand and groan.

"Come on, Allegra." The guy named Tim places a hand in the center of my back. "Take a shot with us." He leans forward to flag down the bartender.

Tequila shots are ordered, and I gratefully accept the one pressed into my hand. "Just one," I warn. My call with Genevieve is on my mind and I don't want to mess that up because I was drinking with a bunch of soccer fans I'll never see again.

"To Barcelona." Tim holds up his glass.

I roll my eyes and take the shot, grinning as the strong alcohol burns a trail down my throat.

"I don't get it," Tim's friend comments, shaking his head. "What idiot left a beautiful woman like you all alone in a pub?"

I take a swig of my beer and look up mid-swallow to see Derek's livid expression.

I choke on my beer as Derek cuts through the huddle. Tim's friend pats my back as I cough into my fist.

"She's not alone. She's with me," Derek bites out, smacking a hand across his chest. It's not violent, per se, but it certainly speaks to a short fuse.

Tim puffs out his chest, annoyed, until he realizes who Derek is. Then his expression falls, and he narrows his eyes at me. His friend jerks his hand away from my back.

My choking under control, I clear my throat, and take a sip of beer.

"We were just—" Tim starts.

"Leaving," Derek's voice cuts in.

He steps in front of my barstool, cutting off my connection with Tim. He plants one hand in the center of the bar and squares off with my soccer-loving friends. "You, not her," he clarifies.

Tim's expression pales as he gestures to the other side of the bar. "Man, we had no idea. Derek Reiner. Jesus, I'm a big fan. I—" He pauses to give me dirty look. What the hell is that supposed to mean? "I'm sorry." Tim hurries away, his two friends right behind him.

"Pussy," Derek mutters before glaring at me. "I thought you understood the rules."

My eyebrows nearly fly off my forehead. "The rules?"

Derek's mouth thins. He shifts his weight and the skull on the back of his hand winks. "About men."

I snort, incredulous laughter bubbling from my mouth. "Are you kidding me? I wasn't going to bring him home. Remember? If anything, I would have—"

"Don't finish that sentence," he cuts me off, his eyes glinting. Derek tilts his head, considering me. "This is going to be a long summer, Stellina."

I breathe in sharply as he casually drops the nickname he gave me years ago. After ignoring me in the studio, to serving me a riddle in the car, to running off the nice guys who chatted with me after he and the band bounced, I'm more than confused. I'm annoyed. And exhausted.

"If this is going to be a problem for you"—I gesture between us—"I'll find another place to crash."

"I didn't say that."

"You haven't said much of anything that makes any damn sense," I snap back, losing my cool.

Frustration flares over Derek's expression. The brunette with the most beautiful hair I've ever seen reappears at his side. She slips her hand in his. "You coming?" she purrs as she tugs him toward the dark corridor we arrived through.

Derek gives me one last look, one filled with conflicting emotions and absolutely no shame. No remorse or regret. Just an edge of that barely concealed anger. He shakes his head once before following the brunette.

I polish off my beer and call it a night.

With women taking body shots off Mav's abs, Levi lost in conversation, and Derek probably fucking the brunette in a bathroom stall, or worse, having gone home with her, I'm drained.

I toss my last twenty-dollar bill on the table with plates

of untouched food, and slip from the pub. Pulling up Google maps, I walk back to the brownstone, beyond grateful it's nearby and Mav shared the lock code with me earlier.

Once I'm inside, I change into a blouse and pull up my hair. I set up my laptop in the kitchen and jot down some notes.

When the Zoom call comes through, I'm ready.

"Hi, Allegra. I'm Genevieve Yaeger, but please, call me Vivi."

"Great to meet you, Vivi. Thanks for connecting with me." I smile at the gorgeous blonde on screen.

She waves a hand. "The Byrne Family have been huge supporters of Maybelle's House and I know Mckenna is considering a career in law. She says you're very passionate about social justice initiatives."

"I am. I just arrived in Boston and hope to gain some hands-on experience this summer, interning with an NGO or doing outreach and advocacy work..." I explain my hopes for the summer. Vivi listens attentively, only interrupting to ask a thoughtful question.

By the time we wrap up our conversation, I'm buzzing with excitement. I knew coming to Boston was the right decision. But with Vivi's generous offer to connect me to other like-minded peers and introduce me to various programs happening in the city, it feels more tangible. Solid.

My issues with Levi, my frustrations with Derek, fade into the background. I miss my brother and I've never stopped thinking about Derek and that kiss. But I'm here for me and my future.

No one is going to distract me from my goal.

Not even an infuriating rockstar with whiskey eyes and a devilish smirk.

FOUR
DEREK

Dark brown strands lace through my fingertips and I give a tug. The woman's mouth slides off my cock and I sigh. This isn't going to fucking work. As much as I want this chick to suck me off and obliterate my thoughts, they keep circling back to Allegra.

"I gotta take a beat, babe," I tell her, pulling her up. I grab the back of her head and kiss her hard on the mouth, just to placate her. "See you around."

"I, uh..." Her gaze is wide, her mouth still open like a fish's. "Yeah. Okay. Call me?"

"Bet," I agree, knowing I'll never dial her digits. Hell, I don't even think I got her number.

Leaving her alone in the bathroom stall, I head back into the bar. My eyes zero in on the booth and I swear when I see it's empty, save for half a pitcher of beer and some sweet potato fries.

I swing around, my eyes searching for Allegra. I clock Levi on a barstool, some girl caged between his knees, her mouth on his neck. And Mav is laid out on the bar, a woman taking a shot of vodka off his stomach.

Panic begins to crawl up my throat. Where the hell is she? Did she meet someone else? Go home with that blond douchebag?

As my thoughts spiral, erratic and concerned, I grasp the back of my neck. I scan slower this time but don't see Allegra. Her purse is gone from the booth.

I pull out my phone and wince when I realize I don't have her number.

Is this how the whole summer is going to go? Me half-crazed with worry and her purposely pushing my damn buttons?

Stepping to Levi, I pull him away from the girl marking the shit out of his neck. "Where's your sister?"

"Huh?" He swings cloudy eyes in my direction.

I repeat my question and he jolts, squinting at the empty booth.

Losing my patience, I release him and stalk to the entrance of the pub. Ignoring the whispers that kick up as I pass, I push open the double doors and leave through the main entrance, anger and adrenaline pumping in my veins.

Our security, led by a former Army Ranger named Drew, and our driver, Alfred, will be pissed but right now, I don't consider their reactions.

All thoughts of the brunette have also evaporated. Now, my thoughts are singularly focused on Allegra. And how I'm going to teach her a lesson when I see her. Like, what the fuck happened to the buddy system? And tell someone when you're leaving a damn bar.

I snort humorlessly, pinching the bridge of my nose. It's bullshit because me, Mav, Levi, and Jameson haven't done that shit since we were sixteen-year-old punks, green.

I never worried about them; never gave their nightly

whereabouts a second thought. But with Stellina, I want to know everything.

Except she's not my Stellina. She's Levi's little sister and right now, we don't know what the hell made her come to Boston. Why does she want to stay here for the summer when it's the last chill summer before her senior year?

What is Allegra Rousell up to?

I arrive at the brownstone and dash up the porch steps, ready to burst inside and holler her name.

But when I get inside, I freeze. I listen. I take a beat to calm the adrenaline coursing through my body. Taking the stairs quietly, as if I'm going to catch Allegra breaking the first rule, I stop outside her bedroom door.

The lights are on but it's quiet inside. Too quiet.

I push the door open gently and peer inside.

Something inside of me softens when I see her, curled up on her side. Her hands are folded beneath her chin, her long eyelashes casting shadows on the curve of her cheek. She looks sweet and innocent in sleep, more like the seventeen-year-old girl I kissed.

I stand in the doorframe, studying her. Then I realize how fucking creepy that is. She's still a kid, only twenty-one years old. Blowing out a deep breath, I flip off her light and close her bedroom door.

Then, I fling myself into a cold shower.

I need to pull my shit together and stop thinking about Allegra.

THE FOLLOWING MORNING, Allegra sips coffee at the butcher block kitchen island looking fresh-faced and wide awake, especially compared to hungover-as-fuck Levi and Mav. Since I cut out early, I'm feeling pretty good myself.

"You need to call Mom and Dad," Levi lectures when I enter the kitchen.

Allegra blows on her coffee, staring at the ripples in her mug, instead of replying.

Levi sighs. "I'm serious, A. You need a plan."

She looks up. "I need a job."

Levi closes his eyes and drags his fingers through his hair, looking exhausted, irritated, and overwhelmed.

I fight back a grin.

"What kind of job?" Mav asks, biting into a doughnut one of his secret admirers delivered this morning.

Allegra sighs, her expression wistful.

I drop onto a barstool, wanting to hear her response. What does she want out of life? What does she care about?

"Something that helps people," she replies. "I spoke with one of the partners of the Harrison Foundation last night. I'm going to swing by Maybelle's House this week." She references a woman's shelter and my stomach twists.

I remember Maybelle's House from back in the day. When I was a hungry, snot-nosed, little kid hugging my mother's legs and begging her to never leave me behind.

She didn't that time. It wasn't until years later that she slipped away, tying off our relationship and discarding me as quickly as a used condom.

I shake my head. Of course, Allegra wants to help others. That would be her first thought.

I knew she was special the night I met her. Even though she's matured, grown up, during the last four years, I like that she still holds that flicker of innocence, that purity. My little star.

I clear my throat to tamp down the unexpected emotion that bubbles up. What the hell is wrong with me?

Allegra, with her tempting curves and soulful eyes, is a distraction. The band is supposed to hit the recording studio hard this summer before we leave for our European tour. I don't have time to daydream about a sweetheart with big brown eyes. My name's not Jameson.

"Good start," Mav replies enthusiastically.

Is he into her? I narrow my eyes at Mav, but his gaze is focused on Allegra.

"I volunteered while at UCLA. Tutoring refugees and recently arrived immigrants in English, making lunches at a soup kitchen, I even hung out with some retired priests." She laughs and ducks her head. "I just want to do something that *matters*, you know?"

"What about women's rights?" Mav asks. "Or the foster system?"

I stifle an internal groan. I know where this is going, and I don't like it.

"What about it?" Levi asks curiously.

"I'd love to work on social issues," Allegra says, grinning at Mav like he fucking solved the issue of homelessness in American cities.

Mav looks at me. "You should introduce her to Dre."

"Who's Dre?" Allegra asks.

"He's Reign's fos—" Mav begins to spill pieces of my past I don't share.

"He's a guy I know," I interject, scowling at Mav.

An apologetic look crosses his face, and he holds up his hands.

Fuck. I sigh, scrubbing a hand over my face. "I don't know, man."

Mav gives Allegra another damn smile. "I'll introduce you to Dre. Let me hit him up. He runs a group home for kids. A lot of them are transitioning in and out of foster care as well. He does an awesome job and runs some cool sports programs for the kids too."

"Really?" Allegra leans over the island, her interest piqued. "That's incredible. I'd love to be part of an initiative like that. Thank you, Mav."

Anger burns through me, and I try to squash is. Am I really going to be pissed at Mav for helping Allegra out? I could introduce her to Dre, but hold back because…

Because I don't fucking want her to know those pieces of my past. My time in foster care, while not a secret, isn't something I advertise. Everything prior to my fame has mostly been buried and I don't talk about that shit. I don't talk about the trouble Dre and I kicked up, or how it went sideways real fucking fast.

I don't want anyone, especially Allegra, to know that while I catapulted into stardom, Dre, my foster brother, shivered on fucking street corners.

Mav taps on his phone screen, oblivious to the emotional turmoil twisting my mind down back alleys I hate to venture down.

"That would be so cool, Mav. I really want to do something I care about, to be part of something bigger than myself," Allegra continues, letting on just how naïve she is.

Her pure, idealistic outlook angers me. Hasn't she learned anything at college? Living away from her family? Hasn't any experience hardened her enough to offer the protection of basic street smarts?

"I thought about law school," she adds, talking about the Law School Admissions Test. "I think my roommate, Mckenna, is going to go."

Levi tunes in, clearly surprised by Allegra's plans.

And I fucking war with myself. Caught between wanting to harden her up so life doesn't spit her out and keep her safe so her compassionate worldview doesn't implode.

It makes no damn sense. None of my feelings are normal. In fact, I feel emotionally distraught, something I've worked hard to tamp down over the years.

"He can meet with you today!" Mav fist pumps the air, his eyes glued to his phone.

Allegra smiles and my heart nearly stops. God, she's fucking breathtaking. "Thank you!" Her hands clamp to the sides of her head. "I need to fix my hair."

Levi rolls his eyes and Mav laughs. "I can walk you over to—"

"I'll take you," I cut in.

Mav gives me a look I ignore.

"I haven't seen Dre in a minute. Where's she meeting him?" I direct this to Mav.

He sighs. "Java House. At two."

I smirk at Allegra. "Be ready to go around 1:30 p.m."

"Absolutely, I will be." Another fucking smile for Mav. "I appreciate it, Mav."

"Anytime, A," he says, using her brother's nickname for her.

Her smile widens.

Levi points at her. "If this works out, you call Mom and Dad. You tell them you have a plan—a responsible one that aligns with your school shit."

Allegra chuckles. "Promise." She makes an X over her heart like a schoolgirl.

I scoff but my chest twists at her cuteness. "Be ready on time."

"I will," she promises.

Annoyed and unsure what to do about it, I grab one of Mav's doughnuts and exit the kitchen.

FIVE
ALLEGRA

I smooth my palms over my jeans and turn sideways to check out my ass in the mirror Mav hung on the inside of his closet door.

I grin. These work. The jeans hug my curves nicely and paired with a short-sleeved white button-down and simple white sneakers, I look put-together enough to meet Dre.

I really want this opportunity. While Vivi mentioned a plethora of volunteer options, they seemed more removed than working one-on-one with kids. While logic dictates I choose a job that pays, I really want to pursue work that fills my emotional cup. Something that guides my next steps.

Plus, I don't want to head home to my parents. Without a job, I'm not sure if my brother will let me crash all summer. Levi's relationship with our parents is tenuous and he doesn't want to give them any more reasons to pretend he doesn't exist.

It shouldn't bother me that Mav jumped in to help before my brother, but it does. Levi's lack of support hurts.

"Ready?" Knuckles rap against the doorframe.

I turn and meet Derek's gaze. "Ready."

"You look fine." He scowls. "You don't need to impress Dre. He'll be into you because you're smart, not because you show your tits."

At his crass words, my eyes dart back to my reflection in the mirror. Just to piss him off, I unbutton another button on my shirt and shoot Derek a look. He scoffs.

I grin. "I'm ready."

He jerks his head to the side. "Let's go."

I follow him down the stairs. Right before we clear his front door, he tugs on a Boston Hawks baseball cap, pulling it low over his eyebrows.

I snort. "That's your disguise?"

He shrugs and holds the door open for me.

"I didn't take you for a hockey fan," I remark as I slip past him. The material of his T-shirt, plain white, grazes my arm and that alone makes me shiver. I shake my head to clear it but his proximity, the scent of his cologne—masculine with a hint of soap underneath—and the heat of his body, messes with my senses.

Does he ever think about that night? Does he remember the stars?

"I'm not." His tone is sharp and with it, my thoughts disperse. He falls into step beside me as we skip down the steps and onto the sidewalk, turning toward the coffee shop. "The girl who does some of our cover art, designs our merch, dates one of the players. She's constantly pawning Hawks shit off on me and swiping Clovers merch in the process."

I chuckle. "I like her already."

He glances down, a pinch between his brows. "Yeah, you would like Claire."

"So, how do you know Dre?" I ask, curious about this guy from Derek's past. Not that I understood much, but the vibe between Derek and Mav was weird at breakfast.

He averts his gaze and I know there's history Derek doesn't want to talk about. Prior to our kiss, I scoured gossip magazines for information about Derek. You'd think I could just ask Levi but even though my brother and I were closer in my youth, he would've found my questioning strange or worse, intrusive.

Still, there wasn't a ton of information. Just that Derek was born in Roxbury, a Boston neighborhood, on March 18. His dad was never in the picture, his mom gave him up at some point, and he aged out of the foster care system at eighteen. Subsequently, he poured all his energy and finances into The Burnt Clovers.

That's. It.

So, I'm curious. I stare up at him, noting the slight scruff that covers his neck and the lower portion of his face. His hands fist, the tats on his knuckles straining. His jaw tightens. Other than that, he gives nothing away. His expression is smooth, his eyes aloof.

"Don't get any ideas, Allegra. You're not his type," Derek mutters.

Humiliation, followed by a swell of anger, burns through me, but I conceal it. "Too bad; he could be *mine*."

Derek's neck snaps toward me at that remark.

I sigh heavily. "But I really just want a job, Reign."

He jerks when I use his popular moniker instead of Derek.

"Not looking for a date," I tack on. "At least, not yet."

Derek sighs and runs his palm over his face. We walk in silence for a few moments, a thread of tension pulling taut between us. My nerves are on high alert, my body tuned in to his every move. I'm hyperaware of Derek's presence—his scent, the annoyed clicks he makes in the back of his throat, the heaviness of his gaze when he glances my way.

Even if my body is a traitor, I keep my eyes focused straight ahead. Put one foot in front of the other. Don't ease the moment by offering up mindless chatter, the way I usually do. This time, I'm not letting Derek off the hook. If I don't stand my ground, The Burnt Clovers will eat me alive.

Derek sighs heavily and I fight the urge to smile.

"We go way back. Knew him since before music." He turns at the corner, increasing his pace. I scurry to catch up to him.

"Oh. What—"

"You think you'll go back to school in the fall?" he cuts me off, piercing me with a look.

I pause, my mouth dropping open. Narrowing my eyes, I search for words. Words I don't have because I have no idea what my plan is. I have no idea what the hell I'm doing past today. This moment. Securing this job and figuring out what comes next.

Derek slows his pace, but his eyes don't leave mine. His expression turns curious, the glint of frustration gone as he waits for my response.

What does he want me to say? What does he expect from me?

Am I supposed to confide *things* in him like that night, so long ago?

I sigh. "I don't know."

Derek blinks. Once, slowly. And in that moment, he hardens. His curiosity seeps into nonchalance. The pebble of concern expands into a boulder of indifference.

"Right," he agrees, resuming his earlier pace. "Come on. You don't want to be late."

I trail behind him, trying to make sense of what transpired between us. Is there anything soft and sweet still there? Can we at least be friends?

Can Derek and I be anything at all?

Another block passes and then, Derek's pulling a door open for me and I'm sliding into a chic coffee bar, the atmosphere eclectic, the air perfumed with the aroma of coffee.

A guy sitting at a back table, clad in cut-off sweat shorts, Jordan dunks, and a starter cap, stands halfway and salutes us.

I grin and lift a hand in greeting.

I got this. I may not have a college degree or years of experience, but I'm enthusiastic, sincere, and wonderful with kids.

As I step forward to introduce myself to Dre, Derek's hand lands in the center of my back. His fingers splay wide, his thumb and pinky nearly grazing my ribs. "Good luck." His voice is low, his tone sharp.

But my body relaxes under his touch. I want to press back against it and melt into him.

Gah! Traitorous body.

Derek's fingertips dig into my skin for half a second before his hand is gone. Instantly, I miss his touch. Immediately, I want him to touch me again.

"What's good, man?" Derek greets Dre.

Dre shuffles forward and slaps Derek on the back. When he pulls away, he lifts his chin in my direction. His eyes bounce from me to Derek and back again.

"She your girl?" Dre asks. He's looking at me, but his question is directed toward Derek.

My palms feel sweaty, and I wipe them on the thighs of my jeans.

Derek hesitates and I work a swallow.

Dre narrows his eyes, his gaze flipping to Derek. Something transpires between them. A silent conversation had through their eyes and small facial movements I can't make sense of.

"This is Allegra," Derek says finally.

I roll my lips together to keep from laughing. Derek will never claim me, but he doesn't want any other guy to call dibs either. I see you, Reign.

"Levi's baby sister," he tacks on.

This time, I snicker.

Dre snorts, a deep sound in the back of his throat. "Fuck," he mutters low. Then, he turns to me and grins, his expression changing in an instant. I recognize the natural charm he exudes, the warmth he turns my way. He holds out a hand. "Good to meet you, Allegra."

I place my palm in his, shaking. "Nice to meet you too."

Dre chuckles. Derek scowls. I bite my bottom lip.

Dre's smile widens and he cocks his head toward the coffee bar. "Want a coffee?"

"Sure," I say, keeping my gaze trained on the barista.

"See you later, man," Dre says to Derek, effectively dismissing him. "I'll walk Allegra home."

A muscle in Derek's jaw pops and his hands tighten. I can tell he hates this idea, but I don't speak up and after a moment, Derek mutters under his breath.

"Say what?" Dre asks, his eyes gleaming playfully.

"Said I'll take a coffee too, fucker," Derek spits back.

Dre cracks up and leads us toward the bar where we order a round of coffees.

"I CAN'T BELIEVE he offered me a job on the spot!" I squeal as Derek and I walk back to the brownstone.

The corner of his mouth lifts, like he's debating smiling, but falls flat before it can curve all the way. "I can. You're passionate about this."

I frown. "How do you know? You couldn't hear our conversation." At first, it irked me that Derek stayed throughout my interview with Dre but now, I'm glad to walk home beside him, reveling in my good fortune.

"I could tell," he offers, gesturing his hands wildly. "You were animated, even across the coffee shop."

I chuckle and swat at him with the back of my hand. My knuckles collide with the hard muscle of his abdomen and Derek sucks in a breath. The sound warms my cheeks and I recall that night. The stars. My first kiss.

Gah!

Ducking my head, I murmur, "Well, enthusiasm counts for something, right?"

Derek smirks, a chuckle falling from his mouth. "Yeah, Stellina. Enthusiasm counts."

I look up sharply at his casual use of my nickname, the one only he calls me. But this time, Derek keeps his eyes trained on the brownstone, his expression aloof, save for a hint of playfulness in his dark eyes.

"I can do this, Derek," I say, wanting him to know that I'm treating this opportunity seriously. That this type of work matters to me.

His eyes shift to mine, all amusement gone. His expression is severe, his lips drawn in a line, his eyes piercing mine. Searching.

My steps falter as I wait for his words. That tension pulls between us again, tight. Desperate.

Derek blinks. "I know, Allegra. You can do anything."

Then, he walks faster, and I try to keep pace with him. We don't speak for the rest of the walk home.

SIX
DEREK

Derek—

Got another email from the man claiming to be your father. His story sounds legit. You sure you don't want me to set up a call? Email is attached for your reference.

Let me know.

—Jess

I roll my eyes at my manager's message. I've received a handful of similar notes, with similar attachments, for nine months now. Same sob story. Same guy—a Derek Madden. Same bullshit.

And guess what? I'm not buying.

Not interested.

I type the one sentence before hitting send and deleting the email, attachment included. Since The Burnt Clovers blew up, I've gotten emails, DMs, and phone calls from tons of long-lost family members, crawling out of the woodwork like termites. Cockroaches.

Where the hell were they when I got put in the system? What were they doing when my stomach was growling so damn loudly, it woke me up in the middle of the night? Or when the outline of a man's palm was repeatedly branded into my skin by mottled bruising that never fully healed before the next one appeared?

I slam my laptop closed.

The only consistent family I've had in my life has been Dre and the guys in the band. More recently, I'd include our lawyer, Aiden Hardsin, manager Jess, and publicist Kimberly. Hard stop.

Still, on holidays, they all have a place to call home. Even Levi who has made burning bridges with his family a favorite pastime, has parents who would welcome him with open arms if he made the effort.

I haven't heard from my strung-out mother, Judy, in so long, years, that sometimes I wonder if she's still alive. Would I know if she died? Would anyone contact me? Would I feel differently?

I doubt it.

"Hey!" Mav knocks on my door before pushing it open and popping his head in. "Allegra got the job."

"Yeah," I say. Like she wasn't going to get it. She's so damn enthusiastic, Dre would have been thick to pass her over. And Dre Ruiz is as sharp as they come.

"We're going out to celebrate."

I narrow my eyes. "Who's we?"

"Me and A." Mav leans against the doorframe casually. His familiar use of her nickname A, the same one Levi calls her, pisses me off.

I clench the underside of my desk. "Levi?"

"Off getting his dick sucked."

"Right." Should've seen that coming. Levi's been borderline out of control lately. The usual suspects—drinking and drugs—the way most of our kind, musicians, find themselves. But Levi's also fucking addicted to sex.

"Wanna come?" Mav offers.

"Sure," I agree, standing up and wiping my palms along the thighs of my jeans. No way am I letting Mav take Allegra out for drinks on his own. He'll leave her high and dry when a hot girl with an ass catches his eye. Or, worse, he'll get sloppy drunk and make a move on Allegra.

Anger vibrates through my veins at the thought. I need to pull myself together. Allegra Rousell is Levi's sister. She's young and enthusiastic and wants to help people.

The last thing she needs is to live in this house with the likes of us. We're wild and rough and un-fucking-couth. And yet, I don't want Allegra anywhere else in Boston.

I pinch the bridge of my nose.

"Tired?" Mav guesses.

"Could use a drink," I say.

He nods. "Get dressed."

"Where we going?"

"Budapest," he names a popular club.

I change quickly, pulling on a pair of black jeans and a soft, charcoal T-shirt that probably costs more than most people's monthly rent. Gotta thank Kimberly for the last shopping haul she did.

Mav tosses me a Boston Hawks baseball cap. "To blend," Mav reminds me. "It's just till we get there."

Nodding, I pull on the stupid cap. The Hawks are a powerhouse team but a few of the players and I have had some run-ins over the years. Mostly, I don't see eye to eye with their left winger, Easton Scotch. But the messed-up shit I had going on with his girl, Claire, was way before she got together with him. And she designed our last two album covers so all in all, I'd say we're cool.

Mav snickers and snaps a quick photo. "For Claire."

I flip him the middle finger and he laughs harder. "Let's go."

I follow him out of my bedroom and down the stairs.

My breath gets stuck in my throat when I see her, idling by the front door. She's changed from earlier, her professional, but casual, ensemble replaced with torn-up jeans and a cropped top that clings to her breasts and shows off her smooth, toned abdomen.

"That's what you're wearing?" I sound like Levi. Actually, I sound worse. Fucking accusatory.

Allegra laughs and fiddles with her long hair. Her gaze darts to Mav. "Should I wear a lace bralette instead?"

Mav cracks up before giving Allegra's hip a squeeze. "Wear whatever you want, babe. You look hot as fuck," Mav tells her the truth. I hate that he can say it so easily. I hate that he can be so damn honest with his feelings all the time, offering unfiltered versions of his thoughts. "If you weren't my roommate, I'd try to get with you. But I don't shit where I sleep."

"Fuck," I growl, wanting to wring Mav's skinny neck.

"It's shit where you eat," Allegra corrects him. But she's chuckling. Her dark brown eyes lighten with sprinkles of sage. "Would you really try to kick it with me, Mav?"

My throat burns at the question, and I shoot daggers at my bandmate, waiting for his answer, which better be a hell fucking no.

Mav laughs and tucks Allegra into his chest. His glare finds my eyes over her head. "Know it, baby girl. Don't listen to anything Reign says. He's a cranky little bitch, is all."

I heave out a sigh.

Mav blows me a kiss and turns toward the door, his arm still around Allegra.

I swear silently and lock the door before sliding into the front seat of the black Escalade. Alfred drops us at the back entrance of Budapest.

Before Mav reaches the door, it swings open, and we're waved inside. We follow a guy until we arrive at a VIP table in a roped-off section, high-end bottles of Clase Azul Tequila and Beluga Vodka already waiting with a bevy of mixers.

"Wow." Allegra whistles, stopping in her tracks to take in the spread. Her sudden halt causes my chest to collide with her petite frame.

To keep her from stumbling, I grip her hip. But she's not at risk of falling over. What does she do? The little vixen grinds her ass against me before shooting me a sassy smirk over her shoulder.

What the fuck is that?

I drop my hold instantly and take a seat.

Why does she keep messing with me?

I need her to be unsure around me. I need her to put up a wall. Because even though I'll want to smash it down with my fist and beat my chest like a goddamn caveman, it will force me to be realistic.

I want to treat her right; the way she deserves to be treated. The only way I'm capable of doing that is by staying away. Apart. Separate.

And Allegra is making that increasingly difficult. Damn near impossible.

When she turns her doe eyes on mine, I yearn to reach for her in a way I've never felt before. It's as if my body is tuned into hers. My concern fixated on her well-being.

And fuck if it's not hard to ignore that shit.

I grip the bottle of vodka, pretending to study it, as Allegra dips into the booth beside Mav.

Maverick grins and tips his head toward the alcohol on the table. "For you."

"You didn't have to do this," Allegra murmurs.

She's speaking so softly, I shouldn't hear her over the music. But I do. I hear every syllable that drops from her mouth.

I clear my throat and toss one arm over the back of the booth. Lean back.

"Vodka or tequila?" Mav asks.

"Tequila." Allegra rolls her lips together. She sits closer to the edge of the seat, perching, to look out over the dance floor.

Her eyes gleam as she takes in the gyrating bodies. The women are dressed in scraps of fabric. Men feel them up shamelessly. Alcohol flows freely. Drugs circulate.

I swallow the bitterness that coats my taste buds, but the sourness remains. This isn't the type of place Allegra should be in and yet, here she is, gratefully accepting the shot glass filled to the brim with tequila.

Mav passes me one and I take it reluctantly.

"To your new job and to the best fucking summer," Mav announces, holding up his glass.

Allegra beams. "Cheers." She clinks her glass against Mav's, droplets of tequila dripping down her fingers, traveling to her wrist.

Mav swipes a lime, already dipped in salt, but before he can hold it out to Allegra, he fumbles it. Laughing, he takes his shot straight, hissing loudly as the alcohol hits his throat.

Allegra tosses the tequila back in one go, her slender neck on full display as the tequila rolls down her throat. She shivers as she swallows and my cock stiffens at the visual, at the thought of her swallowing my—

No! I screw my eyes closed.

Mav's gym bag. Levi's obsession with ketchup on eggs. The stench of sweat on the tour bus. The shape of Simon's hand in the center of my back, spanning between my ribs.

Images of awful, vivid memories swirl in my mind as I try to get my shit under wraps. I can't sport a fucking boner for Allegra Rousell in the middle of a damn club.

I exhale slowly. Shakily.

Allegra looks uncertain for a heartbeat and then, without realizing what I'm doing, or the stupid implications of my actions, I'm there. Holding a lime wedge sprinkled with salt to her full lips. Feeling her exhale ripple over my knuckles.

Allegra glances up, her eyes dark chocolate now. Ninety-percent cacao. They hold mine and I feel the intensity of her presence blow through me like a tornado, shaking everything up inside me and tossing it down in all the wrong fucking places.

"Bite." My voice is low. Gruff. Affected.

Her lips part and her perfectly straight teeth bite into the lime wedge. Citrus scents the air. Tiny droplets of lime spray over my index finger.

She sucks the lime so fucking innocently, with her eyes latched on mine, that I want to pick her up, throw her over my shoulder, and carry her out of Budapest so no other man, or woman, in here has the opportunity to see her like this.

Vulnerable. Sexy. Fucking beguiling.

"Thatta girl." Mav thumps her on the back, and I pull the lime away, discarding it on the table as I sit back down.

I take my shot easily, without wincing. Tequila goes down like water these days. For good measure, I pour a second shot and down that too.

Then, I turn my focus to the shitshow taking place on

the dance floor. Anything to redirect my thoughts. To get my senses under control. To stop fixating on the only woman in here I *can't* have.

I may be a son of a bitch, but I won't be the guy who dims Allegra's brightness.

At least, not tonight.

SEVEN
ALLEGRA

"Allegra Rousell, what the hell are you doing here?" Cynthia bumps into me from the side and I stumble.

A guy I don't know catches my arm and keeps me upright, his hand sweaty, his hold firm. He makes sure I'm not going to fall before turning back to the group of friends he's dancing with.

Blue lights flicker across the bodies in the center of the dance floor and smoke wafts around, making everything hazy. It's a delicate balance between ethereal and raunchy but I'm two shots of tequila down the whimsical path so I throw my arms around my oldest frenemy and exclaim, "Cynthia!"

She laughs and wraps me in a hug. Her signature perfume, Viktor&Rolf Flowerbomb, tickles my nostrils. I used to be envious, in high school, that her mom let her wear perfume and eyeliner while I was clad in pressed khakis and crisp white button-downs. It used to hurt, the way I seemed invisible beside my oldest friend. Guys would check her out, their gazes passing right over me. By senior year, if a boy talked to me at school, I assumed it was to snag

Cynthia's phone number or get some info on who she was currently hooking up with.

Our relationship has always been a gentle push and pull. A delicate battle of wills where I rarely asserted mine and she naturally overpowered. But the familiarity of that perfume, the years of history between us, the buzz of tequila in my bloodstream, and the flash of dancing lights have me sinking into her embrace and holding on for long seconds.

"You good?" She frowns when she pulls back, her eyes narrowed.

"I'm great!" I announce, waving an arm wildly.

"When'd you get into town?" She looks around me, probably searching for Levi.

"Friday." I point to the VIP booth where Derek is glaring at me like I'm ruining his life. His jaw is tight to the point of painful and his eyes are hard and flat, like river rocks.

Cynthia smiles. "It's good to see you. Why didn't you call me?"

I shrug. "Just got back and it's been a shitshow."

She reins back at my profanity, and I chuckle. Cynthia and I have seen each other at Christmas holidays and a few times in the summer, but we haven't spent much time together since high school graduation. I'm not the same naïve goody-goody I used to be.

"Your parents?" she guesses.

I shrug again. I don't want to talk about my parents. Tomorrow, I'll call them to tell them my plans. Right now, I'm celebrating my new job, the start of my new life. Having direction. Any mention of Mom and Dad will damper my good vibes.

"Where's Levi?" Cynthia shakes my wrist, her eyes trained on the VIP section.

"He didn't come. I'm here with Mav and Reign," I say coolly, tossing out Derek's nickname.

My eyes are trained on Cynthia's face, so I don't miss the flash of jealousy that strikes her features. With blonde curls and blue eyes, Cynthia always was the prettiest girl in our class.

She snorts. "What'd he do? Pawn you off on his friends?" Pretty with a poisonous tongue.

The hurtful words slam into me but I'm tipsy. And I'm not the same Allegra I was when she kissed my crush on my birthday, or confided in my mom that I had a secret makeup stash, or broke the news to Levi, before me, that I was moving to California and attending college at UCLA.

"Nah, they wanted to take me out to celebrate." I don't offer more information and let that sentence dangle in the space between us.

"What—?"

"I better find Mav," I cut her off. Tilt my head and grip her shoulder. "So good to see you, Cyn. Hope we can hang more this summer." Then, I'm moving through the sweaty bodies until I spot my roommate.

His tongue is plunged down some redhead's throat, her micro mini essentially flashing us all her goods.

Jesus.

Rolling my eyes, I move back toward the VIP section. But when I look up, Derek is there, holding out my purse.

"Ready to go." He says it like a statement, and I know he's been ready. Just sitting there, watching me, and biding his time because he wouldn't leave me alone at a club the way Mav has no issue doing.

"Yeah." I settle the strap of my purse across my chest.

Derek takes my fingers loosely in his, guiding me out of the club through the same maze of corridors and low lighting we took when we entered. When we exit into the dark alley, a black Escalade is idling.

Derek pulls open the back door wordlessly and waits for me to slip inside before climbing in after me. The second the door shuts, the SUV is moving, smoothly pulling onto a main road, and directing us home.

"She's still trouble," Derek offers gruffly.

I whip my head toward his, studying his profile. "Who?" I ask, even though I know he's talking about Cynthia.

The only other night I've hung out with Derek was the night I turned seventeen. It was at a bonfire in my hometown that Derek pressed his mouth to mine. *After* I saw Cynthia kissing my long-time crush. *After* my supposed best friend encouraged me to take my shot with the baseball star.

"She's jealous of you," Derek continues, not bothering to say her name.

I scoff. Yeah, right. Cynthia has always outshone me, all sparkle next to my dullness.

Derek snorts and shakes his head, as my response irks him.

I yawn, wanting to shake off this strange, almost serious vibe. Tonight was supposed to be fun. Since I ran into Cynthia, my euphoria, mixed with exhaustion, plunged me into a weird headspace.

"Too big for it," he mutters, his words reminiscent of that long-ago night at the bonfire. *You're too big for this. You're going to outgrow this life.*

Maybe he was right. Then. But now... "We're in Boston, not small-town Massachusetts," I remind him.

He glances at me, his dark eyes glimmering in the soft moonlight. "Yeah, and Cynthia is still the mean girl from high school. Don't get pulled into her shit, Allegra. You've already outgrown it."

"I have to call my parents tomorrow," I confess.

He studies my expression. His eyes searching, his lips pressed together.

My heart rate nearly doubles at his long perusal of my features. What does Derek see when he looks at me? What thoughts circle his mind?

I press my palms together, slip them in between my knees, and wait for his words.

My throat is dry, partly from tequila shots but mostly from Derek's unnerving gaze. *Say something!*

"What do you want, Stellina?" Derek sounds almost pained as he asks the question. His voice is raspy, wet sand mixed with shredded seashells, and it skates over my skin like sea glass, smooth with the potential to cut.

His eyes bleed, dark and desperate and dangerous.

"Why'd you really come here?" he tacks on.

I shiver from the intensity radiating off him. His presence expands, eating up the oxygen in the SUV until I'm nearly panting for breath, my chest rising and falling faster.

"I want..." my voice falters, my words breathy and needy.

Derek turns into me, pressing his chest into mine, swallowing what little air is left as he pins me against the seat of the car. "What do you want?" he growls.

His breath fans over my face. My nipples pebble at the weight of his chest pressed against mine. I squeeze my knees together, my trapped hands now between my inner thighs. They tremble as my limbs feel heavy, achy, with a need I've only experienced a handful of times.

"Tell me," Derek demands.

I drag my eyes up from his mouth, his parted lips and

straight, sharp teeth, to the expanding recklessness in his irises.

Is he going to kiss me? I lift my chin in a silent dare and Derek closes his eyes, anguish twisting his mouth.

Then, he's off me, pressed against the door of the SUV, his eyes glued to the passing houses outside the window.

"You shouldn't have come back," he sneers.

My galloping heart rate comes to an abrupt halt at the anger in his voice.

You shouldn't have come back.

He really doesn't want me here. Just like Levi. All I am to these guys, to their band, is a massive inconvenience. An issue to handle.

I roll my lips together. Untuck my hands and wipe my sweaty palms along my thighs.

What did I think was going to happen? Levi doesn't care. Derek doesn't see me as anything more than Levi's kid sister. He's not going to attach the same value to a basic kiss from four years ago when he's been with women all over the country. All over the world.

Embarrassment floods my body and I turn away, training my gaze out my window and the world beyond.

Harboring a crush on Derek all these years was naïve. Hoping that Levi and I would instantly reconnect when we've both changed was short-sighted.

But I don't regret coming to Boston.

I have a job.

The thought flickers to the forefront of my mind.

And a place to live.

I sneak a glance at the back of Derek's head. Silent fury rolls off his tense shoulders and hard edges.

You have a summer.

A summer to figure out my future. A summer to find my path.

I want...to belong.

I twist my face back toward the window as a tear trails down my cheek. It's all I've ever wanted and yet, I'm still *apart*.

But I'm here.

Maybe Derek's right and I shouldn't have come back, but I did. I have one summer to prove him and everyone else wrong.

EIGHT
DEREK

Dre: Your girl's got a heart of gold.

I toss my phone down as soon as I read Dre's message. He isn't wrong and yet, the fact that he spends time with Allegra each day is annoying. Don't get me wrong; I'm happy for Allegra. It's great that she's figuring out her passion, putting her heart of gold to good use.

But does it have to be under Dre's tutelage?

Does it have to be in the same streets I got kicked around at a young age?

Does she see the grimy faces of little kids, with bruises on their cheeks and caked blood on their lips, and wonder: what kind of parents treat their children like this? Let them live in these conditions? Forget about them altogether?

Did Dre tell her about the dad I never knew? Or the mom who liked chasing a high more than she did her toddler?

I screw my eyes closed and shake my head, kicking thoughts of my early years from my mind.

No. Dre doesn't share other people's stories. I know this

and yet, she's too fucking close to aspects of my life I don't want her to know. Memories I don't want to think about.

It's been a week since we celebrated Allegra's new gig and every morning since, she's been gone before I amble down the stairs in the morning. The French press Levi likes to drink when he rolls out of bed is already brewed and waiting. Her one coffee mug and small breakfast plate washed and stacked in the drying rack beside the sink.

Our cleaner Eleanor has commented five times already how nice it is to have a woman in the house. How Allegra's presence alone has made our bachelor pad tidier.

I've barely seen Allegra since last weekend and now, Dre brings her up like she's some familiar, regular presence in his life.

It's irksome, is all.

Dre: Want to teach a music class at the house next week?

Huh? I pause, my thumb hovering over the screen of my phone. Dre's never asked me to come hang at the group home before, probably because he knew I'd say no. When I look at those kids, with their too big eyes and too hopeful grins, I see a version of myself I'm better off forgetting.

Dre: Allegra's idea. She was going to ask her brother but...

Fuck. I grimace. Of course it was Allegra's idea. If she asks Levi, he'll say yes, and Dre knows it will gut me if Levi shows up for her, for him, for those kids, instead of me.

Me: I'll do it.

Dre: Sweet! I'll message you some dates and times.

I shake my head, relieved that Dre doesn't flip me some bullshit, just to gloat.

Dre: But I see how it is. When it's Allegra's idea, it's a good one...

Nope, my thought came too soon. The fucker can't help himself.

Me: Fuck off.

Dre: (laughing emoji)

I toss my phone on my bed, not in the mood for Dre's jokes. I haven't stepped foot inside the group home since Dre took it over years ago. That weekend, I moved furniture. I built bookcases. I helped make up beds and organize toys.

When those kids arrived, there were smiles and laughter and peals of delight. But I couldn't witness it. Not when I know what's waiting for most of them on the other side. Once you age out, you're on your own and the world isn't kind to a foster kid with no family. It's rough and oftentimes cruel.

Dre knows that better than most and the fact that he's committed his career, his life, to serving kids like us boggles my mind. I admire it and I respect it, but I don't fucking understand it. Living through that shit once was enough for me.

Now, I'm going to walk through that door, see those wide eyes, and make those kids feel for an hour. Make them hope and wish and dream.

It's fucking dangerous. For the kids and for me.

Dropping my towel from around my hips, I pull on a clean T-shirt and ripped jeans. I push thoughts of Dre's kids far from my mind and focus on what I do best, music.

Today's recording session was tough, with Levi wanting to switch up the chords. Mav had thoughts on the lyrics I wrote. Jameson was distracted, checking his phone every five seconds. At this rate, we won't finish our album before we leave for our European tour and that shit isn't sitting right with me.

If I can just get these lyrics right.
You vanished like daybreak,
Lost stars and forgotten night.
You haunt me like a shadow,
Clingy and relentless.
You haunt me like her.

I mentally flip through the lyrics, my mind snagging on *lost stars and forgotten night*. Something isn't working and no matter how many times I turn the words over in my mind, I can't pinpoint what's amiss.

"Yo." Levi knocks on my door before pushing inside and ending my mental loop.

I flip my chin at him, my wet hair brushing against my forehead. I swipe it back and wait for him to say his piece.

Levi sighs. "You still pissed about the session today?"

"I'm not pissed," I mutter. I'm pissed as fuck. *Lost stars and...*and what?

Levi snorts. "Yeah, okay." He walks farther into my bedroom and sits on a chair I've got in the corner. It's usually piled high with discarded clothing, but Eleanor came today. "We're a band, Reign. Just because you're lead guy—"

"I'm not—"

"Shut up." Levi smirks. "We all know you reign." He chuckles at his own dumb joke. "And that's all gravy. But it doesn't mean you dictate everything. You gotta hear me out. Hear Mav out. Not all my ideas suck. Not all his lyrics are shit."

I breathe out heavily, my nostrils flaring. While Levi may technically be correct... "We still stuck to the originals in the end."

He shrugs. "Yeah. Your chords worked better. Now we know because we *tried* something different."

"I knew from the jump," I remind him. Does he think I didn't test different chords before writing the song? Does he think I half-ass my songwriting?

I don't. Out of all my bandmates, I spend the most time in the studio. The most time with a pen and paper, writing lyrics, creating music. And I will get this song exactly the way I want it, or it won't end up on our album.

"You're a stubborn, cocky motherfucker."

Fact. "And?"

Levi shakes his head and stands from the chair. By his demeanor, not angry but not agreeable, I can tell he's said his piece and is moving onto the next thing.

Levi Rousell is a talented musician, but music doesn't own his soul the way it owns mine. Music saved my life. It gave me a real shot in the cruel, dark world I aged into. It's my survival guide.

For Levi, it was just a convenient way out from under his family's thumb. Mr. and Mrs. Rousell had a future vision for Levi that he never wanted to embrace. The Burnt Clovers are a convenient "fuck you" to his parents and small town.

Since we made it big, Levi's more interested in fucking women and snorting coke than he is in jamming. As much as I don't understand it, I try not to judge him. Too harshly.

I lift my eyebrows, waiting for him to get to his next point.

"There's a party at Flip's tonight."

"Fuck Flip," I mutter, referencing one of Mav's stupid friends. "He nearly got busted moving coke last month."

Levi shrugs, like the thought of years in prison doesn't faze him. Maybe he thinks he's untouchable. I've witnessed it before. People get too comfortable, whether in their wealth or in their depravity. They think nothing can happen to them or nothing worse can occur.

But it can. You can always fall from grace.

And there's always a level deeper than what you think is rock bottom.

Levi Rousell from his strait-laced upbringing, in his too-small town, just doesn't know that.

Neither does his sister.

I scrub a palm over my face at the thought of Allegra.

"What's your sister doing tonight?" I ask before I can help myself.

Levi narrows his eyes. "Why?"

I shrug. "Don't you think you should, I don't know, check in with her? Spend some time with her. She's here for you."

One side of his mouth lifts and curls but his expression is sinister. Skeptical. "Nah, man, A's here because she doesn't know what the hell she's doing with her life and knew I wouldn't turn her away." He spreads an arm wide, as if to encompass our brownstone. "This arrangement gives her some breathing room, yeah?"

"No, man, that's not true," I say automatically. "Allegra loves you. Always has."

Levi's forehead furrows. "Always has? You've fucking met her once, Reign. What, you talked to her extensively at her seventeenth birthday party?"

"I'm just saying, she seems legit. Sincere. Said she was trying to connect with you…"

"Changed my number. Too many girls got a hold of it."

"And you didn't give it to your sister?" I can't hide the edge of disbelief from my tone. If I had a sister, I'd make sure she always had access to me. Hell, if I had any family, I'd make sure to stay connected.

"Why do you care so much?" Levi asks, studying me.

"Don't. I'm just making an observation."

"Yeah, well here's another one. Since my sister showed up, you've been keeping to yourself, bailing on nights out. Not hooking up, not drinking... What gives, Reign?" His eyes narrow further as his expression twists. "Do you have a thing for my sister?"

Surprise slams into me. Not at his statement, but that dense Levi would put two and two together when he's usually half-baked and fully oblivious. So, I laugh. I tip my head back and bellow, swearing colorfully as my bark cuts the air. "Are you outta your fucking mind? Levi, Allegra's a fucking baby. She's the last girl I'd be interested in since I like my women experienced. You know, as a woman."

Relief fills his expression. His confusion dissipates; his former line of questioning forgotten. "Right. Yeah, man, of course. All right, let's head to Flip's. Come on, it'll be fun."

Shaking my head, I force a chuckle. "Yeah, okay. Let's do it," I agree, knowing I can't beg off now.

Levi hits me on the shoulder as he moves past. "Be ready around nine."

"'Kay," I agree as he opens my bedroom door wider.

The second she comes into view she averts her gaze. But I see the hurt that clouds her irises. I catch the disappointment that lines her mouth.

"A!" Levi announces, like he's surprised to see her. The realization that she overheard our conversation doesn't register on his expression as he slugs an arm around her shoulders. "You talk to Mom and Dad yet?"

I wince as her mouth twists and her eyebrows shoot up in disbelief. That's the question he led with? Levi's self-centeredness has gotten worse over the past few years as his share of women, drugs, and fame has grown.

But I never thought I'd see him extend it to his baby sister. Years ago, he spoke of her with a fondness, a closeness, that made me jealous.

"Tonight," she responds. Hardens her tone. "I'll call them tonight."

"Good." Levi smacks a kiss to the side of her head. He points at me. "Nine p.m., brother." Then he moves toward his bedroom.

I stand still, my gaze concentrated on the bold brunette I know I hurt. But Allegra doesn't show it. Instead, she lifts her chin in my direction and narrows her eyes. She's waiting for me to...what? Apologize? That's not gonna happen. My fingers beg to curl into fists, but I keep my palms steady. I don't move. Instead, I train cool, calculated eyes on Allegra.

She meets my gaze for a heartbeat, her expression defiant. Her cheeks are painted pink with anger. Her dark eyes are large and deep and fucking fearless. Then, she flips me half-a-mysterious smirk. It's mocking and challenging and so unlike the girl I first met that I frown in response.

Allegra passes my bedroom en route to her own and closes the door with a snick.

"Fuck." I tip my head back and lift my gaze to the sky, as if calling on a deity I don't believe in for answers I know won't come.

I stopped believing in good shit years ago. Allegra Rousell is good shit.

Confusing as hell and a total mindfuck. She's not for me to hope for.

Because hope has the potential to blossom, and I don't. All I'll ever be is withered leaves, disintegrating in her bloom.

NINE
ALLEGRA

I'm relieved Mav is already out for the night when I close the door to our shared bedroom.

I know Levi and Derek's conversation wasn't meant for my ears. But coming home from a long day washing sheets, cleaning bedrooms, adding personal touches, and making sandwiches to welcome four kids to their new home left me drained.

Overhearing what Derek and Levi think of me guts me.

A's here because she doesn't know what the hell she's doing with her life and knew I wouldn't turn her away.

How callous has Levi become? How could he think that of me? When we were younger, I worshipped him, and he looked out for me. Always. Now, I don't recognize my brother and the realization that he changed his phone number and didn't bother telling me cuts. Does he care about me at all?

Allegra's a fucking baby. She's the last girl I'd be interested in since I like my women experienced.

Fine, I'm not experienced. Or the same age as Derek.

But seven years isn't that big of an age gap and I'm not exactly a virgin.

My limbs vibrate with a silent fury. Missing my roommates and best friends and needing to clear my mind, I pull up our group chat.

Me: Levi sucks.

Nova: I'd still do him.

Me: EW.

Ivy: NOVA! He's her brother.

Nova: And a rock god with tortured eyes...

Kenny: What'd he do now?

Me: Nothing! That's the problem. He has done nothing to spend time with me or reconnect. He thinks I'm here because I have no other options.

Nova: Gross. Guessing he doesn't know that you could have gone abroad this summer?

Ivy: PARIS!

Kenny: Or interned in LA?

Ivy: Are you sure you don't want to re-enroll for fall? Just as a backup...

Me: I love the work I'm doing here. Even though things with Levi are strained, I'm happy I came to Boston.

Kenny: Good! Focus on that... Focus on your future.

Nova: And Reign???????

Ivy: PLEASE give us something good.

Me: He likes his women "experienced."

Nova: (six vomit face emojis)

Kenny: What's that even mean?

Me: That I'm clearly lacking...

Kenny: Not true.

Me: (three shrugging emojis)

Nova: You need to go out!

Ivy: Agreed. You need a girls' night...

Nova: And not with Cynthia.
Ivy: Right. New friends.
Me: Are they going to just fall in my lap?
Nova: Gotta put yourself out there, babe.
Ivy: You're good at connecting with people!
Nova: CONNECT WITH GOOD MEN!
Me: I'm calling my parents tonight.
Nova: Does that have to be tonight?
Ivy: Can't you make a friend first?
Kenny: Good luck, A! Message if you need us.
Me: Always.
Nova: (four leaf clover emoji)
Me: (red heart emoji)

Knowing that Levi and Derek are heading out soon, and wanting to avoid them, I throw myself in a hot shower and let the steam soothe my body. Allow the tension in my neck to seep away and let my shoulders relax. When I'm finished, I tug on a pair of pajama bottoms I stole from the cellist who took my virginity freshman year and an oversized T-shirt from Ivy's softball team. I comb out my hair, letting it air dry, as I wander down the quiet hallways.

The house is silent, save for my breathing. I let out a deep exhale and tuck my hair behind my ears. Then I retreat to my bedroom and make the phone call I've been putting off for over a week.

"Hello?" Mom answers on the first ring.

"Hi, Mom," I say.

"Allegra!" I hear the surprise, the tentative smile, in her tone.

"How are you?"

"Good. Fine. How are you? How are your roommates? How's LA in the summer?"

My lips curl of their own accord. As much as I don't

understand my parents, I know they love me. It's just that their version of me and who I really am are two different people that no longer align. "You know how I took a leave of absence...?"

Mom sighs. "Allegra, I know we talked about that, but did you really? You're so close to finishing your degree. And after making us all worry by running away to California, can't you stay and finish what you went there to do?"

I run a hand through my hair, try to organize my thoughts. I can do this; I can tell Mom the truth. "Well, I'm taking some time," I forge ahead. "I'm in Boston."

"Boston!" she gasps. "When did you arrive? Who are you staying with? Is it Cynthia? Or one of the girls from school. Isn't Mckenna Byrne from Boston?" She references Kenny whose parents live close by.

"Mom," I say quietly, my tone an admission of guilt. A soft confession.

Silence fills the line for several heartbeats. I pull in a deep breath and focus on keeping my breathing even. Controlled. Calm.

Disappointing my family and hurting the people I love isn't in my nature. I used to be a full-out people pleaser and spent years resisting the flicker of rebellion that flares to life whenever I'm at a crossroads. I push back only when I feel it's necessary. Attending college instead of choosing to marry. Insisting on UCLA over the local university.

But I don't relish it. Not like Levi.

My fingertips tingle and my stomach clenches, painful. Nausea gathers at the base of my throat and a throb begins in my temples. I roll my lips together to keep my words trapped.

I hate hurting my parents. I despise disappointing my community, the town that loved, supported, and raised me. Coming up short, constantly, cuts. Invisible remorse oozes from my pores but I will not apologize for my choices. I won't second-guess my decision to be here.

"Don't let him corrupt you, Allegra." Her voice is sharp. "I know you love your brother—"

"So do you," I remind her. I bite down on my tongue. Why do I always defend him? Why do I rush to Levi's rescue when he thinks so little of me?

She doesn't know what the hell she's doing with her life and knew I wouldn't turn her away.

"He's lost, Allegra," Mom hisses, anger rounding out her words. "He's not the boy I raised. Not by a long shot."

I gather saliva in my mouth, work a swallow down my sandpaper throat. Forge ahead. "I'm staying at the brownstone."

"No!"

"For the summer."

"Come home, Allegra. I'll talk to your father. He'll allow you to stay here," Mom pleads.

I roll my lips together. Dad hasn't spoken to me in over a year. To him, his children have made decisions he can't accept. As such, he's stopped recognizing Levi and me altogether. But not Mom. At her core, she loves us too much to let us go entirely.

"I'm working with kids in the foster system," I offer, knowing that any social justice initiative will soothe some of her fears for my soul.

"Wh—you are?"

"Yes." I smile, running my hand over the top of my head. Encouraged by her interest, I tell Mom about Dre, about the group home, about Vivi and Maybelle's House.

"That's good work, Allegra," Mom comments.

"It really is, Mom. I, I'm figuring things out. I'm discovering my calling. My purpose."

"I understand," she admits quietly. "But Allegra, you're to be a wife. A mother. To have a family and—"

"I'm not ready," I interject, not adding that I may never be ready. The life my parents envisioned for me is never one I wanted. I never connected with the boys from Church, who took up their fathers' work when they laid it down, who stepped into lives that have already been determined for them without question.

If I question everything, how can I live my life with a man who accepts all? What kind of love would we share? What kind of family would we foster?

My stomach hallows out at the thought. No, I'm not meant to live in my small town.

You're too big for this.

Derek has grown into Reign. And he's wrong about a lot. But on my seventeenth birthday, he told me the truth.

You're going to outgrow this life, Allegra.

On that topic, he was right.

"Maybe we could have lunch one day? You could come to the city and meet me. Even see Levi, if you want..." I extend the olive branch. Hope surges through my body and I try to tamp it down. Breathe. Controlled and calm.

Mom is quiet for a long time, her accelerated breathing filling the line.

"May? Who's on the phone?" Dad's voice reverberates in the background.

"Good-bye, Allegra," Mom whispers. "May God be with you."

She disconnects the call and my face, my body, my heart collapses.

She won't meet me. She won't cross my father or the

rules he laid out for her. When he cut us off, he expected Mom to follow suit.

I let out a shaky breath and place down my phone.

I miss my mom. I miss our family.

Don't burn your bridge home to Mom and Dad's for me, A. I'm not worth it.

Maybe Levi is right, but I'm not here only for him. I'm here for me too. And I am worth it.

Still, hurt rushes forward, drowning my momentary hope. The disappointments of the day, the loneliness I've been staving off, rises. I sit down and let it crest over me, pull me under.

I sob, with shaking shoulders and trembling hands. But it's silent. Contained. My anguished cries don't pierce the still air.

Instead, the hurt flows out in big, fat, tears. The pain lessens with twisted intestines and a rapidly galloping heart. My desperation rushes from my body, first, in gut-wrenching swells that overwhelm me. Then, in a stream of whispers I mouth to myself. Words of despair coupled with the prayers of my upbringing, the comfortable foundation I can never erase because it keeps me tethered to the parents I love, to the community I remember, to the life I outgrew but don't want to discount.

Finally, my hurt and shame, my disappointment and heartache, dissipates. My tears cease, my skin dries. My face feels too tight, my eyes puffy and scratchy. But I pull in a lungful of air and exhale loudly, expelling the tension from my shoulders and neck.

My head throbs so I make my way to the kitchen. Take an ibuprofen and drink a glass of water. I grab a book of poetry I love, a gift from Kenny, and curl into a corner of the couch in the living room. I turn on the electric fireplace to enjoy the dancing of flames. They hypnotize me, transporting me to a night so long ago, I should have forgotten it by now.

But the night Derek Reiner kissed me, my world opened up. For the first time, new possibilities, the ones that only existed on the edges of my reality, in half-formed shadows, seemed feasible. Believable.

When he pressed his mouth to mine, he gave me more than hope. He gave me the confidence to believe in myself enough to try. To dip my toe into the endless options that life has to offer and then, lose myself in the current as it swept me away.

To find my purpose. To move across the country. To study topics I'd never been exposed to. To make the friendships of my heart and explore my feelings with a cellist whose music rivaled any Church performance.

She's the last girl I'd be interested in since I like my women experienced.

He has no idea who I've become. No one, not even me, fully grasps the potential I'm capable of.

Shaking my head, I lose myself in the well-worn pages of verse I adore. I read until exhaustion weighs down my eyelids. Snuggling deeper under the blanket, the flames kicking up shadows on the wall, I close my eyes, and allow myself to rest.

TEN
DEREK

My toes catches on the lip of the threshold as I stumble inside.

"You good?" Drew asks. Tonight, since we went out in a group, Drew and Samson tagged along.

"Yeah, man." I wave him off and shut the front door. Splaying my hand against the wall, I keep myself upright.

Fuck. My head spins and my vision blurs. I blink to clear my eyes.

Fucking Flip and his parties. The drugs are always pure as hell. The women, so goddamn sexy, they look photoshopped. Smooth skin, glittering eyes, curves that beg to be rocked. Grasped. Bodies meant for fucking.

I drop my head back against the wall.

And none of them get under my skin, mentally work me up, the way Allegra does.

None of those girls hold a fucking candle to a little star like you.

It was true four years ago and it's still true now.

Jesus. I smack a palm against my cheek, as if I could slap the deranged, wayward thoughts from my mind.

Do not think about Allegra Rousell.

She's a fucking kid. She's Levi's sister. She's good and authentic and fucking perfect.

I make my way toward the kitchen, toeing off my shoes as I go. I toss my phone and wallet onto the butcher block island and nearly have a heart attack when I look up.

"Jesus!" I wheeze, a hand coming to the center of my chest. "What the hell are you doing in here? In the goddamn dark?" I bark.

Allegra stands quietly beside the stove, her hand wrapped around the handle of a mug. The kettle is heating on the stove and she's waiting patiently, quietly, for the whistle to wheeze.

"Just making tea," she replies softly. She turns her attention back to the kettle, dismissing me and my anger.

I frown, trying to figure out what's wrong, what's off, in this scenario.

Allegra, recently clad in clothes that highlight her tight body, is swimming in baggy pajama pants and a T-shirt that hits her mid-thigh. Her long hair is damp in some places, gently curling in others.

"Allegra," my voice is hard.

She drags her eyes to mine, slowly turning her neck.

I swear when I note the puffiness of her eyelids, the red that rings her chocolate irises. "Were you crying?" I sound accusatory.

She sighs, flips off the gas, and pours steaming water into her mug. "Good night, Derek." She picks up her mug and makes to move past me.

"Wait." I snatch her wrist. She fumbles the mug and places it on the island, shaking out her fingers as a droplet of hot water lands on the back of her hand. My eyebrows pull together. "Are you okay?"

She snorts and shakes her hand again. "Fine. It barely got me."

"Not the tea," I growl.

She gives me her eyes and the melancholy in their depths is crushing. I feel it to my core, a quiet pain, a desperate hurt, a kind of lost I've spent most of my life existing in.

But Allegra isn't supposed to experience that.

Allegra is too big, too good, too fucking special for the jaded world I know.

"What happened?" My voice sounds half-strangled.

She shakes her head. "Nothing. What would happen in your beautiful home to the most inexperienced woman you know?"

I rear back at the glint of anger in her eyes, at the crack of her words.

But I'm too drunk to sort out her meaning. Fuck, am I blitzed. I hang my head, trying to shore up my defenses, trying to formulate something half intelligent to say.

Her wrist feels delicate in my grasp. Flimsy. Fragile.

Her scent, light and soft and natural, messes with my cognitive abilities. Her presence tosses me off-balance. The heat of her skin soaks into my palm and I want to feel it everywhere. Want to hold her, press my body up against hers, bury myself inside.

Fuck. I shake my head. *What the hell am I thinking?*

She moves to pull away and my neck snaps up, my eyes finding hers.

Allegra pauses, gasping at whatever she reads on my face.

Can she see the desperation I feel whenever she's near? Can she tell I'm losing my fucking mind, knowing that she's down the hall from my bedroom, her soft breathing a lullaby I never knew existed?

"Do you have any idea what you do to me?" I voice the question aloud. Too intoxicated, too tired, to care that I'm crossing the line I drew in the sand.

She lets out a shaky exhale and her breath, warm and sweet, trails over my chin. Her eyes hold mine. In their depths, a question swims and a challenge sparks.

I reach out. Drag my fingers through her silky strands, gently push them behind her ear, trace her delicate earlobe with the pad of my thumb.

Allegra shivers and I feel it travel through my veins like an electric shock.

"Allegra." Her name is a moan on my lips. "Stellina."

She bites her bottom lip and I audibly groan. She looks at me with naked curiosity, with a bite of hunger, in her gaze. A sweet face, a soft mouth and pleading, begging eyes.

And I fucking snap.

I step into her space, forcing her to shuffle back a step.

"Do you know that every woman I looked at tonight, I saw you?" I growl, advancing on her.

Her mouth drops open in a surprised O.

I snort. "Want to see that face for a different reason."

Her eyebrows bend, confusion etched in her expression, before they lift in surprise.

I laugh. "Fuck, you're sweet."

Her back collides with the kitchen counter, and I step into her, drop her wrist to grasp her hip. Wrap my hand around her body and sink my fingertips into the extra material of the most hideous fucking pajama pants I've ever seen.

"Why're you dressed like this?" I ask.

She shakes her head, as if she doesn't understand my question.

"Doesn't matter. I still want you, fucking crave you," I admit.

"Reign," she starts, and I hate that she doesn't call me Derek. Especially when she never calls me Reign.

But she's adding the distance we both know we need.

"You mad at me, Stellina?" I tip my head, studying her face, memorizing the shape of her mouth.

"I heard you. And Levi." Her voice is scratchy, uncomfortable with the memory of her eavesdropping.

"You should've kept walking."

"You shouldn't have said it in the first place." She swats my hand off her hip and straightens her spine.

The movement presses her breasts, soft swells I want to touch, to hold, to test the weight and rub circles around her nipples, into my chest. I lean into her, desperate to feel those pebbled peaks through the thin fabric of her T-shirt.

She gasps and I grin.

"None of those girls hold a fucking candle to a little star like you," I slur, a memory, a reminder, a promise.

Then, I kiss her.

I take her parted lips between mine, press my arousal into her abdomen, dig my fingers into the dip of her waist, and kiss her.

She melts under my touch, and I groan in satisfaction. Stellina still harbors something for me. And fuck if I don't want to devour her.

In a moment of weakness, lost in her softness, I kiss Allegra Rousell like she doesn't have the power to upend my fucking life.

Like I won't destroy her.

I kiss her hard, taking her mouth, nipping at her bottom lip, plunging my tongue into the depths of hers to tangle and taste and take.

Her fingers find my shoulders and curl into the material of my shirt, gripping.

I bend her like a bow, curving my body over hers, wanting to possess every fucking part of her.

Our kiss is sloppy. My mind is all over the damn place. My blood runs hot and my limbs buzz. Desire burns through me, burying reason and destroying logic.

Rational thought flees the kitchen and debased, desperate lust takes over.

Our kiss is passionate and wild. It's heady and confusing and wrong on so many levels.

I drag my hand up her body, my thumb swiping over her right breast, until I cup her cheek and angle her face.

Allegra turns her head quickly, so my mouth lands on her cheek.

"You taste like whiskey," she accuses me.

I snicker. "You taste like want, my little star."

I watch her swallow travel down her throat.

Then, I turn her head back to me. I search her eyes. I don't fucking blink as I lower my mouth to hers. Again, I kiss her.

But this time, it's gentle. It's sweet.

It's so fucking reverent, it scares the hell out of me.

Allegra scares the hell out of me.

Her eyelids flutter closed. Her body slackens against mine. Her chest rises quickly, her heartbeat erratic against my torso.

The front door bangs open.

"Fuck, what a night!" Levi announces his arrival.

Allegra rips her mouth from mine and dips her head, hiding her face.

I swear and step away, letting her go and turning to block her from her brother.

Levi stumbles into the kitchen with Mav close behind.

"That was fucking epic!" He raises one fist in the air.

"He had the Jensen twins," Mav explains, laughing. "You remember them? You fucked them after the concert in Amherst."

I nod, recalling a blurry night with two blondes and too much coke.

Too late, I remember Allegra.

Spinning around, I frown at the empty kitchen.

She's gone.

I glance at the island. So is her tea.

Allegra vanishes and I blink.

My mind clings to the image of her dark eyes and the taste of her mouth.

My palms tingle to feel her curves again.

"Fuck," I mutter.

I want to plunder every part of Allegra's body.

Then I want to shape her whole again.

And that is a big fucking problem. One I need to rectify in the morning, when I can see straight. Think rationally.

Remember my commitment to the band. My promise to myself not to snuff out the brightest star in the sky.

ELEVEN
ALLEGRA

My eyes are still puffy when I wake the next morning. My lips feel swollen.

Running my fingertips over my mouth, excitement travels through my body. My awareness is on high alert, taking stock of every moment of my exchange with Derek last night.

The golden flecks that danced in his chocolate eyes. The firm press of his mouth, demanding, that soon turned soft, sipping from mine. He smelled like whiskey and cologne. He tasted like smoked apples and salvation. His hands knew how to hold me, his grip strong and committed.

It's been four years since Derek Reiner kissed me and right now, my mind recalls every second of that long-ago night. My body craves another encounter with the edgy rockstar.

"Eek!" I squeal, giddy and wide awake now that I confirmed last night wasn't a dream. Last night, Derek offered me comfort and concern after his ugly words gutted me. After Levi's dismissal stung. After Mom and Dad's actions reminded me just how alone and adrift I am.

But, just like last time, when all seemed hopeless, Derek appeared. He reminded me I'm enough; I'm okay. And he kissed my pain away, giving me something a million times better to hold on to.

His mouth. His eyes. His mysterious vibe I can't pin down but want to wrap myself up in. Until we're both lost, together. Wandering, with direction. Kissing, with abandon.

I shiver, a shimmy dancing up my spine as I snuggle deeper under the covers.

I freeze for a moment, listening intently to ensure that Mav isn't sleeping in the bunk below mine. Without his light snore rattling the air, I know I'm alone.

Blissfully alone with my delicious thoughts and achy body. I bite my bottom lip, my fingertips tapping against my lower abdomen, as I close my eyes and remember last night.

The bewildered anger in his eyes when he first spotted me in the kitchen. The tormented agony that bled from his expression when he stepped into me, saying words that lit me up, brighter than the New York City skyline.

Do you know that every woman I looked at tonight, I saw you?

Stellina.

Fuck, you're sweet.

My fingers slide beneath the waistband of the pajama bottoms I slept in, toy with the lacy edge of my pastel panties.

He hovered over me, tall and hard and imposing. My fingers swept along his shoulders, my thumb pressing against the tattoos along his collarbone. A flock of ravens, a burning heart. Derek stole my breath with one dark glance, his smirk twisted, his expression pleading.

For what? I wanted to ask.

But his kiss responded instead.

I slip my hand farther south, my fingers lightly tracing the outline of my lips, light and delicate. Imagining it's Derek's touch, his caress, instead.

His tongue invaded my mouth as my lower back cut into the lip of the countertop. His desire overwhelmed my senses, debasing reason and plunging me into the vortex that he is. All-consuming, omniscient, everything.

The pad of my index finger glides through my slick folds, and I gasp, a needy groan falling from my lips. I do it again, with two fingers this time, and my lower abdomen clenches, the ache between my thighs growing. Gathering my arousal on my fingertips, I press on the bud of nerves, smearing my want over my clit, and moan again.

Derek's hand flexed on my hip. My fingers grasped his shirt. He kissed me hard, his mouth pouring a drug down my throat. One that made me wanton and desperate. One that made me feel and desire and crave.

I rub circles over my clit, increasing the pace. My hips buck once, searching for friction.

The feel of his arousal, sheathed in denim, pressed into my stomach. God, how I wanted him to lift me up, sit me on the edge of the counter, and spread my thighs.

His hand grazed my ribs, one whisper-light touch across my breast. Fuck, if only he'd palmed it, dragged his thumb over my nipple until it pebbled and peaked, a hard nub counteracting his calloused finger.

Using the pads of my fingers, I continue to massage my clit. I've had sex before but I'm the only person who's ever been able to get myself off. To bring myself to a crest that promises to break. A thread that snaps, a spool that unravels.

Derek's rough cheek, his stubble scratchy, coarse

against my soft skin. The sound grated the air, making the particles around us buzz to life. I melted into him. I melted for him.

Please. Please. Please. A silent chant.

You taste like whiskey.

You taste like want, my little star.

My hips pulse upward on their own accord, meeting my fingers in a natural rhythm that curls the tension in my body, pulls it tight, manipulates it expertly. My eyes squeeze closed.

The sound of the bunk bed swaying fills my ears. I sigh loudly, half a gasp, half a moan. I keep the pace, my touches in time with the rhythm of my movements.

I wish it was you, Derek. Banging this bunk bed against the wall. Entering me with abandon. Taking me to peaks I've yet to reach, need you to climb, want you to free-fall from. Beside me. Alone, together.

My fingers are dripping with my arousal. The scent of my want wafts around me and I breathe it in, wishing his scent mingled with it.

Then, he closed his eyes. He angled my head. His thumb swiped over my cheekbone, and he pressed the softest, sweetest kiss against my lips. Intention and promise and care poured from him into me and—

I press my fingertip against my clit one final time and my body detonates.

"Yes," I groan, satisfied. Relieved. Grateful.

My toes curl, my heels digging into the mattress, as the sweetest satisfaction pours through my limbs, rushing like the warmth of sunshine, with the strength of a natural disaster.

"Fuck," I swear, tapping my head back against my pillow.

I remove my hand from my panties, damp with arousal and sweat and a want that threatens to consume me.

"Derek," I say, half wishing he'd hear me.

Half wishing he'd enter my bedroom, pull off his shirt, and climb on top.

My throat is dry, and my inner thighs shake as I regulate my breathing.

None of those girls hold a fucking candle to a little star like you.

MY PERFECT MORNING crashes down the second I enter the kitchen. For a heartbeat, I hover in the doorway, trying to process what I'm seeing.

Derek, shirtless, seated at the kitchen table. His hand is casually gripping a navy mug, the name of the band's last tour stamped on the front. The other guys are milling around.

Mav is across the table, his feet propped up on an empty chair. His blond hair is disheveled, and a hickey mars his neck.

My brother is hungover, his forehead resting on the butcher block as he tries not to slide off the barstool. Beside him, a redhead nibbles on burnt toast.

But it's the woman perched on Derek's lap that steals the breath from my lungs. Her presence, casual and familiar and perfect, plunges an icy fist into the center of my stomach and nails my feet to the spot.

I gasp, shock rocking me to my core.

She's gorgeous. Of course, she is. Long, dark hair that hangs to her waist. It's mussed and twirled, sexy bedhead. Her toenails are polished red, her legs are tanned and bare.

She's dressed in an oversized T-shirt, another piece of band merchandise and the collar is shapeless, slipping off one rounded shoulder as she turns into Derek's frame. She giggles at something he mutters in her ear and presses a palm, with long, slender fingers and the same red polish, against his chest.

She looks at him with moonbeams in her eyes.

Is that how I looked at him last night? With hope? Trust?

I avert my gaze. Study my plain, unpolished, chipped nail beds that haven't had a manicure in months. Not since Nova last polished them.

"Morning, my beauty," Mav greets me.

My head snaps up. I manage a watery smile, careful to avoid Derek's gaze. Oh, but I feel it. He watches me intently, waiting for my reaction. Gauging to see how I respond to the beautiful, half-naked woman perched on his knee like a delicate bird.

Will she fly away? Or make a nest, right here, in the kitchen?

"Morning," I clear my throat.

My brother grunts but doesn't look up. Figures.

I force my feet to move, one foot in front of the other, as I relocate to the French press. I make a mug of coffee. I inhale the rich scent, close my eyes, drop my shoulders.

I'm enough; I'm okay.

"What'd you do last night?" Mav tries again.

"Nothing worth mentioning," I reply, keeping my back to the room, my gaze trained out the window.

Derek snorts but I don't take the bait.

Instead, I turn around calmly, a smile pasted on my face. I tip my head toward the redhead and then the brunette. "My name's Allegra and Levi's my brother." I gesture toward the disappointing lump on the barstool with my mug. "If you need shampoo or anything, help yourself to whatever's in the bathroom."

The redhead grins. "Thanks, babe."

"Yeah," the brunette, I'm guessing her friend, adds. "That's real sweet of you. I'm Jenn and this is Kate." She points at the redhead.

"Nice to meet you. Hope you had a great night." My gaze quickly rolls around the three guys. "And that they let you finish first," I tack on as I move toward the stairs.

Mav chuckles, his hands tapping out a drumbeat on the edge of the table. "Damn, A! Don't call us out like that."

The girls' laughter fills the kitchen as I plant my foot on the first step.

Derek doesn't say anything, but I feel his gaze.

Curious and dark. Frustrated and confused.

I don't turn around, even though I want to.

I don't meet his eyes, even though they hold the answers I seek.

I force myself to keep going, one step in front of the other, until I'm locked in the bathroom. With the shower on and the hot water cascading over me, I scrub my skin with a frustrated fury.

Derek Reiner isn't the same guy from four years ago. He's changed.

Has he?

Maybe he's always been Reign and I just wanted to see him as Derek.

None of those girls hold a fucking candle to a little star like you.

What a fucking liar.

I rinse conditioner from my hair and wash my face.

I won't give him the satisfaction of knowing he's hurt me. Again.

Instead, I hold my head high. I towel off and conceal my misery with makeup. I dress quickly and don't bother calling out a good-bye as I head to work.

The door slams behind me. I breathe in the blue sky and sunshine. Put one foot in front of the other.

Go to work to discover my calling. My purpose.

Because it sure as hell isn't being a plaything for Derek "Reign" Reiner.

TWELVE
DEREK

For the first few weeks of July, I keep my distance from Allegra. Honestly, she makes it easier by spending as much time as possible away from the brownstone.

Allegra throws herself into work with a single-minded determination I can't help but admire. From Dre, I learn about the initiatives she sparks. The collaborations she arranges with Maybelle's House. The fundraising events she volunteers at and her newest friend, a formerly homeless man in his sixties, named Buck.

She also befriends Claire, the girl who does our cover designs, and starts spending nights out with the Boston Hawks Hockey girls, including Vivi who runs Maybelle's House.

As much as her new life, forged without my help or her brother's support, annoys me, I can't dim the flicker of pride that flares. She's doing it. Stellina's brightness is growing and if it continues, unchecked, it'll be enough to light up city streets.

While Allegra is busy finding herself, I follow suit. I

throw myself into the music, into sessions at the studio, into preparations for our upcoming European tour.

The song I can't quit continues to play on a mental loop as I wrestle, day in and day out, with the lyrics. Nothing feels right. In the meantime, I confirm the date I'll do a music lesson with Dre's kids.

I carry on with fucking my sidepiece, the leggy brunette with a splatter of freckles on the bridge of her nose, and mentally pretend she's Allegra. She's nothing but a cheap imitation but right now, it's as close as I can get to the real deal, so I take it.

"A here?" Mav asks as he enters the kitchen.

I slide one headphone off my right ear and glance at him. "What if I was working?"

"You wouldn't be sitting in a common area," he answers easily, reaching into a cabinet and pulling out a bag of pretzels. He drops a handful of twists into his mouth, chomping loudly.

I slide my headphone back on my ear.

"What are you working on?" Mav wonders.

Sighing, I yank the headphones down around my neck. "A song." *The* song! If only I could perfect it; if only it flowed the way I know it's capable of.

"Why are you sitting in the kitchen?" He glances around the bare space, his eyebrows pinched.

I don't want to admit I'm waiting for Allegra to get home. I don't want to voice that she's been spending less and less time in our fold and more time out with Claire and Vivi. More time at Boston Hawks events and Maybelle's House fundraisers. Lunches with Dre and Buck and her work crew; drinks with friends I know nothing about.

"Change of scenery," I murmur.

"Allegra home?"

I shrug, as if to indicate I have no idea.

Mav cracks his neck. "I'm happy for her," he shares, as if I should be interested. Except I am so like a schmuck, I lean forward and pitch an elbow on the butcher block. "She's been here a month and she's already got a friend group. Good girls too. I mean, Claire's a fucking riot."

"Yeah," I agree. Claire Merrick is a cool chick. Even dating Easton Scotch, who is a total douchebag, didn't dim her awesomeness.

"I'm glad she stuck around after you fucked her over," Mav comments.

I roll my eyes. "We don't need to revisit the past. Claire and I were a summer fling. It's not my fault she thought it was more than that."

"It was your fault that you stuck her with a $3,000 bill at Carter's." Mav lifts an eyebrow, calling me out for some stupid shit I did when I bailed on Claire to get high and fuck some chick in the alley behind Boston's best steakhouse.

"I paid her back."

His eyebrow lifts.

"I did. Took a few years but it got sorted and Claire and I are straight. What the fuck is your point?"

Mav chomps another pretzel. "You're in a mood."

I close my eyes, my frustration rising. "We spend too much fucking time together."

His loud chewing echoes in my eardrums.

"The point is, you're obvious as fuck, sitting here, pretending to work when you're really wondering where A's at."

My eyes snap open, a frown twisting my face.

Mav laughs. "So predictable. So, you are wondering?"

"Fuck off."

He laughs again and shoves more pretzels into his mouth. "Just be grateful she's out with a solid girl group."

"She's out with the Hawks girls tonight?" I ask, hating myself for giving Mav the satisfaction of knowing that yes, I am wondering, thinking, worrying about Allegra. Our bandmate's sister.

Mav shrugs and smirks. "She's out somewhere. I just got a workout in with Dre, and he said the staff took off early today. Summer Fridays." Mav gives a little shimmy, being the playful doofus he is.

"Bet."

Mav snorts. "Anyway, I'm going to rinse off. Want some help with that?" He flips his chin at my open laptop.

While Mav has decent ideas, I'm used to working, writing, solo. I like the process of scribbling out thoughts, playing with rhythms and tempos, experimenting with lyrics. And this piece I'm working on, the parts I'm stuck on, are too personal to share yet. I'm still making sense of it. I don't know how to wade through my mess of thoughts with an audience, especially a loud chewing one like Mav. "I'm straight, mate. But thanks."

Disappointment clouds his eyes, but he blinks it away.

I peer closer. Did I offend him? "I—"

"No need to explain." He holds up a hand. "Another time."

"Uh, yeah. Sure," I stammer.

Retreating to my bedroom, I toss my laptop on my desk and swipe up my phone. I'm not much of a social media guy but I've got a Finsta account to keep up with what's happening in the world.

I find Allegra's handle @happystar and chuckle.

"See what you did there, Stellina," I murmur, recalling that her name, Allegra, means happy in Italian.

I scroll through her feed. It's mostly photos of her with friends, groups of girls laughing, eating, and posing. There's some of the beach in California, a smattering of popular tourist attractions in Boston, like Paul Revere's House, and foodie pictures.

It's a snapshot of Allegra's life. A window into her world.

I tap on her stories and my eyes narrow as I recognize the bar, Taps, where Allegra is taking a selfie with Claire and one of the Hawks players, Reese Keller.

In the next story, a guy I don't recognize has his arm wrapped around Allegra's waist, a hand splayed on her hip.

"Who the fuck are you?" I mutter, tapping to the next story.

A group taking tequila shots. Caption: *Apparently, this is for @TorstenHansen!*

I roll my eyes. Stupid hockey. Tap for the next photo.

Allegra wearing a Hawks hat, some random kissing her cheek.

Claire, Vivi, and Allegra giggling.

Easton Scotch and the team captain, Austin Merrick, their shot glasses raised in the air.

Allegra sitting on some fuckwad's lap, his palm resting on her upper thigh, his fingers way too close to the seam of her jeans.

"Fuck this," I swear, striding to my closet. I'll change and swing by Taps. Walk in for a beer. It's not like I haven't frequented the bar before. I mean, it's not my spot like it is for the Hawks players, but anyone can grab a beer if they're in the mood.

I press my thumb against the screen to switch to the next story and groan when I realize the group has relocated.

Now, Allegra is sitting in a kitchen barstool at, I'm assuming, one of the Hawks' houses.

"Of course, she's friends with the fucking Hawks," I sneer, tossing my phone onto my bed.

My earlier pride is snuffed out as anger takes root.

Why the hell did she have to befriend the Hawks?

Who are these guys she's hanging with?

Are any of them trying to get with her?

Of course, they are. Any man with a cock would want to stick inside Allegra Rousell. She's a walking wet dream.

I grip the back of my neck, my agitation making me antsy.

Doesn't Levi give a shit that his sister is hanging out with strangers, all around the damn city? Doesn't anyone care about Allegra? Worry about her safety? Display concern over her choices, however sound they may be?

I retrieve my phone and push into the hallway, in desperate need of a distraction. Swiping a finger across the screen, I call up my leggy brunette, who's always down to fuck.

"Hey, Reign," she answers on the first ring.

Predictable. Desperate.

"You around?" I cut to the chase.

"I can be there in fifteen." Her voice is breathless.

"I'll come to you," I say, wanting to get the hell out of my house. Away from reminders, energy, that belong to Allegra.

"Okay," she agrees enthusiastically. Shit, I hope she doesn't think this means something. "It's just sex," I remind her, in case she's reading into it.

"Always," she confirms. Like the idiot I am, I believe her.

She rattles off her address and I slip my phone into the

back pocket of my jeans before bounding down the stairs and out the door.

Then, I head to Jenn's place and fuck her hard. It offers a temporary reprieve, a momentary distraction, a sweet relief.

For an hour, I lose myself in skin and sweat. In moans and curses. In a woman with long brown hair, a tight body, and freckles. A gorgeous woman.

But she's still not the one I want.

THIRTEEN
ALLEGRA

"He's bad news," Boston Hawks Hockey captain, Austin Merrick, confirms.

My new friend, Claire, wrinkles her nose. "He's grown up a lot—"

A chorus of snorts rings out around the table.

"You give him too much credit, babe," her boyfriend Easton kisses her temple.

Claire shrugs and levels me with a look. "Real talk..." She leans closer and drops her voice, allowing the conversation around us to continue in her and Easton's brownstone kitchen. "Reign and I used to..." She widens her eyes to clue me into her meaning. Her gaze shifts to her boyfriend before whipping back to me. "East is *not* a fan."

I chuckle. East looks like he'd want to put Derek through a wall for hitting on his girl.

"I've worked with him for years now, even after our... summer fling." She flicks her wrist, as if she doesn't know what to label their exchange. "And we're cool. He has grown up a bit. But he also left me high and dry with a massive check at Carter's to go screw a woman in an alley and snort coke." She shrugs, as if her story doesn't sound wild and insane and hurtful as hell.

I rear back in surprise, my eyebrows knitting. "He just... left you?"

Rolling her lips together, Claire nods. Her blue eyes narrow as she studies me and she chomps on an end of her blonde waves, like it's a stalk of dried wheat. "Be careful, Allegra. I know you've known Reign and the guys for years but...Derek always chooses Derek. Considering he's one of the most complicated men I've ever met, or worked with, he doesn't really do complicated. Instead, he cuts ties to protect his peace."

I heave out a sigh, recalling Jenn. She and Kate have been at the house for several nights the past week. It's gutting to know that after he kissed me, flipped my world upside down and gave me this spark of hope I haven't felt in years, he went and slept with another woman.

Flaunted her in my face the following morning.

Just to make sure I understand the score. To put me in my place, back where he wants me.

"Yeah," I agree.

"Now, Mav on the other hand..."

I raise my eyebrows expectantly.

"He's good people," Claire laughs. "Obviously." She gestures toward me.

When Mav introduced me to Claire a few weeks ago, I thought he was reaching. Why would the band's designer, the girlfriend of a Hawks player, with a full social life, want to hang with me?

But Claire easily scooped me into her circle, our connection strengthening when we realized we have Vivi in common. Now, I have my own girl group, reminiscent of Kenny and Ivy and Nova.

All thanks to Maverick Tate.

"Yeah, Mav said we'd hit it off," I agree, tucking my hair behind my ear.

"Mav's usually right." Claire points at me. "Another nugget of wisdom as you navigate The Burnt Clovers minefield."

I laugh and lift my glass, clinking it against hers. "Thanks for this, Claire." I gesture around the kitchen.

Some of the team and their girlfriends met for burgers and beers at Taps before hanging here. They included me without question, asking about my life, sharing funny stories, and making me feel like I belong *somewhere*.

"Don't mention it." Claire takes a swig of her wine. Next to her, Easton pops the tab on a sparkling water can and takes a long drink. "We've all been where you are."

"Lost?" I supply, grinning to mask the hurt in my voice. "Untethered and wandering and—"

"Stop!" She places her hand on mine, halting my speech. Tilting her head, she gives me a small smirk. "You're not lost, Allegra. You're figuring out your priorities. You're forging your own path. And that's scary." She bites her bottom lip thoughtfully. "But brave as hell."

I laugh and take another sip of my wine. Next to me, Austin's wife, Chloe, pulls me into conversation.

I hang out with this amazing group of friends, of found family, and wonder why I can't find this level of connection with the Clovers? Save for Mav, I haven't clicked with any of the guys.

If anything, the chasm between Levi and me has widened. Derek confuses me at every turn. Jameson is hardly around.

I could see past that if the guys were at least connecting but from where I'm standing, it feels like the Clovers are reaching a breaking point. One that will either dramatically explode or quietly crumble.

I drain my wineglass.

"A." Levi stops me the following morning before I leave for work.

"Hey," I say, surprised my brother is awake at this time.

His eyes are bloodshot, and his hair is mussed, as if he just rolled from bed. His or someone else's?

Levi clears his throat. "You talk to Mom and Dad?"

I sigh, moving to the French press and pouring a coffee. "I asked Mom to meet me for lunch..."

A flicker of hope crosses my brother's face. It's instant and genuine, and reminiscent of the big brother I used to adore. "And?"

My throat tightens painfully since I know my words will squash his hope. His expression will fall, his expectations will plummet. I clear my throat, choosing my words carefully.

But my hesitation speaks volumes and Levi swears quietly. "She said no, didn't she?"

I nod and touch Levi's wrist. "I'm sorry, Levi."

"Don't be. It is what it is. I didn't think she'd say yes. I mean, to see you, sure. But not me."

"I thought she'd come. To see us both," I admit.

"Really?" Levi cocks his head.

"For a minute there...yeah. I tried calling again but Mom..."

"Won't cross Dad," he supplies.

"Exactly."

Levi heaves out a sigh and takes a swig of his coffee. "I know we haven't spent much time together this summer."

My heart hammers in my eardrums. Is Levi going to... apologize? I grip my coffee mug tighter. Would it change anything?

Yes! If Levi offered me an olive branch, a path forward, to restore our relationship, I'd take it. I miss my brother; I miss my family.

"And that's on me," he admits, surprising us both. "I'm sorry, A."

"Your rejection hurts, Levi," I tell him the truth. "I've been away for three years and it's hard to admit how far apart we've grown in that time. Sometimes..."

"What?" he whispers, his eyes intent on mine. His irises are shaded in remorse, his expression lined with regret. "Say it."

"I don't even recognize you. The partying, the women, the drugs—"

"I've got everything under control, A. It's harmless." He tosses me a smirk, reaching for levity that doesn't exist in this moment.

"It's not," I say, softening my tone. "None of this is harmless." I gesture around the kitchen to imply the brownstone, the band, the fast life they're all living. "You're going to Europe at the end of the summer," I remind him. "When we were kids, we used to dream about what it would be like to visit London. To see the Colosseum in real life. To climb the Eiffel Tower. It seemed magical."

"Yeah."

"I skipped out on studying abroad to come this summer. To try to reconnect with you. And now, you're heading to Europe. You're getting the chance to do all those things we wished for as kids. Instead of appreciating that, you're focused on women and parties and—"

"Come with us," he cuts me off.

I rear back in surprise. "What?"

"Come. To Europe. Come for the tour. Sightsee, do all the things we dreamed up as kids. Climb the Eiffel Tower. I'll be better in Europe, A. More focused. It will give us the chance to reconnect the way we should have this summer."

Hope swirls in my chest, dangerous and delusional. But I want to believe my brother. I want to step into the painting he just created in the space between us. Broad strokes of color, tiny details filled with moments.

London, Rome, Paris. Paris! Our childhood dreams becoming a reality that we could experience together.

Still... "Do you really mean that, Levi?"

He places a hand on his heart, looking hurt. "Yeah, A. I mean that. I miss you too. This summer, fuck, the past few years, they've been crazy. Intense. Fun as hell but...I'm glad you're here. Please, let me make this up to you. Come to Europe."

I sigh. I've always wanted to visit Europe. And now, Levi is offering me the opportunity of a lifetime and I'm hesitating because of Derek! He pops up in my mind, always eager to make an appearance.

Can I handle seeing him with other women, night after night?

Well, it won't be much different from summer in Boston.

But I won't have friends in Europe, bouncing from one city to the next.

Maybe Nova will meet me in Paris? Her dad lives there.

I wonder if Kenny and Ivy would come out too?

"Say yes, A," Levi pleads. He gives me his best puppy

eyes, his sad grimace, a face I recall from a loving childhood spent with a protective brother looking out for me.

I grin and take a massive leap of faith. "Yes."

Levi laughs and pulls me into a hug. "You won't regret it, A. This tour, we'll reconnect. We'll see Europe. We'll be like little kids again."

"Okay," I agree, hugging him back. I want to believe his words and the intention behind them.

I want to have a relationship with my brother.

So, I block out the giant red flag of Derek Reiner. I dismiss the thought that I'm compromising my future to follow Levi overseas. I shut down all the negativity and focus on the positive.

This is a chance to be close to Levi again; this is an opportunity to rebuild our family.

Levi kisses my cheek. "I'm heading to bed, A. I'm glad you're in."

"Me too," I say, and I mean it.

Once Levi leaves, I rinse out my coffee mug and head to work. On my walk over, I text the group.

Me: Plot twist. Levi invited me to Europe! For the tour!

Me: I said yes! I'm going to Europe for the fall. Anyone want to meet me anywhere...

Kenny: ???

Kenny: Are you serious?

Ivy: I hope Mckenna meets you so we can stop running at the crack of dawn.

Nova: I'm in for Paris! We can stay at my dad's. Can you get us backstage passes?

Ivy: She can get you on the tour bus, Nova.

Nova: See you there, Allegra. Send me the dates.

Kenny: Are you sure you want to blow off the semester to go to Europe?

Ivy: She already took a leave of absence...

Nova: Kenny thinks she's going to change her mind and come back.

Me: Mckenna?

Kenny: Sorry. I do. Or I did. It just seems like heading to Europe for the fall isn't part of your plan. I thought this summer was to help you align career goals...

Me: It is.

Kenny: How does that work if you spend four months in Europe?

Nova: Shhhh, Kenny! Stop ruining this for us! It's only four months, A. It's an experience.

Ivy: I'm torn. I see both sides... Did you think this through, Allegra?

"Sorry!" I call out to a man I nearly collide with on the sidewalk. I turn a corner and lean against a building, narrowing my eyes at the stream of messages.

Did I think this through? Barely.

Does Europe further my career goals? I could network while I'm there...

Gah!

Me: Guys, it's a chance to reconnect with Levi.

Kenny: But that's partly why you went to Boston! If he wants this relationship as much as you, shouldn't he compromise?

Shit. My stomach sours and I heave out a sigh. Her words hurt because I recognize the truth in them.

Nova: He can't compromise when he's selling out shows across the pond, Kenny!

Ivy: Just think about it, Allegra. Whatever you decide, we'll support you.

Nova: Right, Mckenna?

Kenny: Of course. I just don't want you to get hurt, Allegra.

Nova: But if you do, I'll fly out to get drunk with you in London.

Nova: Or Paris.

Nova: Or Berlin.

Nova: Or Athens.

Ivy: You're a true friend, Nov.

I snort and swipe a hand across my face.

Me: I'm nearly at work. I'll keep you guys posted.

Ivy: We love you!

"Yo!" Dre hollers when I walk into the house. He's cleaning up from breakfast. The kids are already at camp.

"Hey," I greet him, shaking off my friends' messages and flashing a smile.

"Derek's in for the music lesson on Friday," Dre informs me.

I rear back in surprise. When Dre mentioned Derek would do it instead of Levi, I was skeptical. "Seriously?"

"Seriously," Dre confirms.

Buck tugs on the end of my ponytail. "Want to hang with me in the soup kitchen this morning? Could use your help with the lunch rush."

"Absolutely," I agree.

Dre brushes crumbs from his hands and flips on the sink's faucet. "That'd be great, A. There're some boxes I wanted to bring over to the office but if you're going to the soup kitchen…"

"We'll take them," Buck confirms.

"Awesome. Here, let me show you which ones."

"Okay." I tuck my sunglasses into my small backpack and drop it on the kitchen counter. Then, I follow Dre into a closet that houses inventory and other needed items.

Dre stacks boxes. When he turns to glance at me over his shoulder, the cuff of his T-shirt rides up on the back of his bicep and I pause. The tattoos are small. Black ink pressed into his skin with perfect clarity. A flock of ravens, taking flight up and under his shirtsleeve.

I squint, recalling a similar, no, the same tattoo, beneath Derek's collarbone. I dusted my fingertips across it three weeks ago. I imagined pressing my mouth to it, dragging my tongue over his ink, up the column of his neck, searching for his mouth.

I wince. Yeah, that clearly didn't happen.

"You good?" Dre asks, giving me a strange look.

"Yeah." I shake my head, hoping to clear away thoughts of Derek. Ha! Impossible. I gesture toward his arm. "Just, your tattoo..."

Dre arches an eyebrow.

"Derek has the same one," I comment.

"Yeah," he confirms, plopping the final box on top. Turning, Dre crosses his arms and glances at me, waiting.

"Did you get them together?" I wonder.

He bites the corner of his mouth and snorts. It comes out as a puff of breath, kicking up dust particles off the box tops in the closet. "Something like that."

This time, I lift my eyebrows.

"You should ask Reign."

"I'm asking you," I counter. Frowning, I shake my head. "Derek—"

"Derek?"

"He...confuses me." *And I don't know if I should go on tour with the band or not!*

"Welcome to the club." Dre leans against a shelving unit. He kicks one scuffed sneaker heel against the toe of the other one before meeting my gaze. "Listen, A, you're good people. It's obvious from the second someone meets you."

"Thanks," I say, dragging the word out. That didn't sound like much of a compliment even though the words were kind.

One side of Dre's mouth lifts in a half grin. Falls. "Your heart's unguarded," he continues. "You wear your emotions on your sleeve."

"I—well, that's not my intention," I admit, a defensive edge to my tone.

Dre laughs. He drags his thumb and forefinger across his eyes and pinches the bridge of his nose. "I know. You can't help it."

I shrug.

"Reign, he's got all that shit buried. It's buried so deep, some would claim he doesn't have it—the good, the heart, the emotions—at all."

I frown.

"It's not true," Dre confirms. "He lets it out, lets it all pour right the fuck out, in his music. That's his true love. His passion. That's the place where he's all in, no take backs, no regrets, no do-overs."

I straighten, not liking where Dre is going with this. If I go on tour with the band, will I see a side of Derek I don't know? One I like even less than the bullshit he's currently flipping my way?

"He's not all in with people, babe. Especially not with women." His expression softens. "Even the girls he cares about. Even the good ones with hearts and emotions." He half shrugs to take the sting out of the truths he shares. Pointing at his tattoo, he flicks his bicep. "Reign protects his past. If you've got questions, you need to ask him. All I'll say is, deep down, he's loyal. He's a good friend. But you've gotta peel back a lot of fucking layers before you see it, believe it, fucking trust it." He shakes his head. "Just be careful, A. Heartbreak won't suit you, ya feel me?"

Slowly, I nod. "Yeah." I clear my throat. "I understand." But inside, my stomach sinks. My toes scrunch in my sandals, searching for a stronger grip on the ground. On reality.

I'm not going to Europe for Derek; I'm going for Levi. For our relationship and our family.

Gah! Even though we're barely speaking, Derek is on my mind. An enigma, he draws me in with dark glances. He keeps his hold with subtle promises of more. Of possibility.

Dre's warning levels me because in the center of this storage closet, I realize he's right.

Derek's love is music. Full stop.

And my love is people. Being here, in Boston, has only solidified that.

Derek's a taker. By nature, I'm a giver.

And I'd give all of myself to him until there's nothing left. Until I vanish and he takes over.

Until the ravens circling above pick me apart. Even then, I'd still wish and want and worry for Derek Reiner.

"Come on," Dre says softly, guiding me out of the closet. "You and Buck need to get going."

"Yeah," I agree, nodding but my mind is elsewhere.

I mentally flip through my interactions with Derek since I've arrived. They've all left me unsettled. Confused. Uncertain of where I stand with him.

As the pit of dread in my stomach expands, I wonder if I'll ever move past him. It's laughable because he was never mine.

But he's always belonged to me. I'm his Stellina and he's my first...everything that matters.

Dre sighs. "Talk to him, A."

I glance up through wary eyes and Dre winces. "And say what?"

He looks at me for a beat before shaking his head. "I don't know. The truth?"

I snort.

Dre tucks me under his arm and chuckles.

Outside his office door, we share a hearty laugh that leaves me half in tears and half breathless.

Claire may have been right about my finding my own path and discovering my priorities.

But she was also wrong. I'm not brave.

Brave would be cutting ties with Derek. Instead, I'm scared I'll always carry a torch for him.

That I'll always long for something I'll never have.

Be a little in love with a man who doesn't understand that emotion at all.

No, I'm not brave. I'm terrified.

And now, I'm spending the fall with him in Europe.

FOURTEEN
DEREK

I pluck the guitar strings casually, meeting the eyes of each kid in the room. On the periphery, I feel the sharp gazes of Dre, Allegra, and Buck. Nerves cause my stomach to twist. I pluck out another chord, closing my eyes and letting the music, the feel of my guitar in hand, to soothe me.

Releasing an exhale, I look around the half-moon of kids gathered around me. I'm sitting on a low stool in the center of the group home's living room. The motley crew in front of me boasts a variety of ages, ethnicities, and attitudes.

The little girl with pigtails looks bored and pays more attention to the letters her index finger traces in the thin carpet. The boy beside her, small-boned and sharp-eyed, watches me like a hawk. In the back, a pre-teen glances over from the corner of his eye, curious but not wanting to appear eager.

I snort and shake my head. "Give me a request."

A girl with ginger-colored corkscrews raises her hand politely.

"Teacher's pet." The girl beside her rolls her eyes.

I grin. "Let me hear it, ginger."

Her eyebrows lift and she glances to the girls on either side before she realizes I'm talking to her. "Miley Cyrus's song 'Flowers,' please."

Dre's snicker, concealed as a cough, rings out and I fight the urge to flip him off because, kids.

"You got it," I tell the little girl. Her eyes light up and something weird tugs in my chest. "Hey, what's your name?"

"Sarah," she answers excitedly.

"Great choice, Sarah." Miley may not be my jam but who am I to begrudge Sarah with the corkscrews?

I strum the opening notes and put my own twist on the lyrics, singing for the group. When I'm done, they clap their hands enthusiastically and I chuckle.

"Okay, let's get Sarah up here first. You're gonna learn to play C chord." I gesture for her to come closer and hold out my guitar.

"Me?" she gasps.

"Yep. And we're all going to encourage Sarah," I tell her snarky friends.

As I demonstrate a simple C chord, the kids lean closer. I run through it a few times, helping Sarah position her fingers correctly. Her friends call out a few encouraging words or gentle critiques and slowly, we learn C, Em, and G chords. The kids all take a turn, even the pre-teen that glowers at me.

I grin in response. "What's your name?"

"Jem." He lifts his chin, daring me to poke fun at his name.

"Derek," I reply.

"We all know who you are, man."

"Good. Now I know you too."

He rears back at my response.

"You're in charge of helping the kids practice their chords," I tell him.

"What? Why?" he whines.

"You're the oldest here." I glance at Dre for confirmation and when my friend nods, I push my guitar into Jem's chest. "This is for you. Gotta step up for the younger ones."

He scoffs and opens his mouth to flip me bullshit, but I shut it down.

"Sarah, scootch over. You and Jem are going to learn the beginning of 'Flowers.' Then, Jem's going to help you perfect it before your next lesson."

"You're coming back?" Sarah squeals, genuinely excited.

That weird sensation zips in my chest again. Fuck, these damn kids. I drop my chin. "Yeah, girl. I'll come back."

I ignore Allegra's sharp inhale.

"Come on, Jem! We gotta learn." Sarah pinches Jem's side.

Jem narrows his eyes and in their depths, I read his wariness. Distrust. Kid reminds me of Dre and myself, and I'm drawn to him as much as I detest the shadows in his gaze. He's grown up too fast, seen too much. It's made him hard but at his core, there's a softness. There's that flicker of fucked-up hope.

"Sit down," I instruct. He does.

Then, I teach the group the opening to Miley Cyrus's song. When Sarah gets it right, they all whoop and cheer. Even Jem smiles and nudges her playfully.

I glance over my shoulder and catch Dre's eyes. He lifts his chin in my direction, letting me know that he sees it too. Jem as the hard-ass wannabe; Sarah as the enthusiastic light. Once upon a time, Dre was Jem, and I was Sarah. That was our bond. But when it all fell apart and came back together, Dre searched for good, and I let the darkness reign.

Shaking my head, I turn back to the music group and end our first lesson.

"DIDN'T KNOW you had it in you, Reign," Buck comments.

I snort. "Me neither," I admit. "Thanks for the coffee."

He tips his head in understanding. We're standing on the back porch, watching as Dre runs the kids through a series of soccer drills for some upcoming camp he's conducting. Allegra helps carry out Dre's instructions and gives each kid some one-on-one pointers. I should have bounced by now and yet, I'm still here, watching this group of kids. Reliving parts of my past through shattered lenses.

Some of the bad seems better. Some of the good seems worse. The whole thing is cracked, like a kaleidoscope of shifting shapes and varying colors, in my mind. I can't stop glancing at Jem. And Sarah.

"You're welcome anytime," Buck offers.

"I know. It's just weird."

"It's tough. Coming back."

I give him a look and he hides his grin behind a swig of coffee.

"She doing okay?" I tilt my head toward Allegra.

"More than okay. She's made this summer better, maybe even the best yet, for a lot of these kids." He shakes his head. "No clue where she gets the energy."

I snicker. "Getting tired, old man?"

He laughs. "Can still best you, Reign."

"I know it," I agree, taking a pull of my coffee.

Buck's been Dre's mentor for years. He helped Dre turn the corner, get his life on the up-and-up, and give back to a community who needs him. For every step forward Dre took, I backpedaled. But Buck never held it against me. He still greets me like my fuckup wasn't responsible for Dre shivering on fucking street corners or eating at soup kitchens. He forgives me with the same sincerity as Dre and it hurts.

It guts me to know that these two men still want a failure like me around.

Dre blows his whistle just as I take a sip of my coffee. The sound startles me, and I fumble the cup, swearing when I spill some coffee on my shirt.

Buck chuckles.

Shaking my head, I wait for Dre to wrap up his final pointers. Once the kids are washing up for supper, I head toward him.

"Thanks for coming, man," he says, grasping my fingers and pulling me into a hug that ends with his big bear hand slapping me on the back.

"Yeah," I say, not admitting that I had fun. That it was better than I expected. That Jem and Sarah are going to stick with me.

"See you next week?" he pulls back.

I don't miss the question in his voice. "Yeah." I nod to confirm that I'm in. I'll do music lessons at the group home.

Dre grins.

Allegra steps in our direction.

Dre points at her. "Get out of here, Allegra Rousell. You're off the clock."

She smiles. "See you tomorrow, Dre."

"See you, girl." He smacks my shoulder. "And you."

Then he walks toward Buck on the porch and the two of them disappear inside the house.

I stuff my hands into my pockets and rock back on my heels, studying the brunette beauty infiltrating my thoughts. My dreams. My goddamn life.

She's kept her distance and still, I crave her. Recall the way she tastes, how she feels, the way she makes my blood sing.

"Hungry?" I ask, surprising us both.

Her eyes flare but she slips her hands in the back pockets of her cut-off shorts and appraises me thoughtfully. "I can eat."

FIFTEEN
ALLEGRA

"Where are we going?" I ask as Derek leads me down a tiny alleyway. We parked over two blocks away and as my flip-flop catches on a cobblestone, I slow my pace.

He matches my stride, glancing at me. "I don't come here often but I think you'll like it. The food is good but the vibe, the vibe is chill as hell."

"Okay," I agree, following as he stops outside a cobalt blue door. "Oi! Out here," he hollers.

The door opens a moment later and an elderly woman, with an apron tied around her hips and her silvery-grey hair pinned back in a low bun, beckons us inside. "Sit wherever, Reign."

"Thanks, Lyd," he replies, closing the door.

I pause, drinking in my surroundings. It's not a house, like I originally assumed, but a restaurant, albeit a small one. There are seven tables of varying shapes and sizes, surrounded by chairs or stools or a workbench. Antique lamps dot end tables and a record selection takes up the back wall. A phonograph plays throwback songs and I grin at Derek.

"This is cool," I say, placing my little backpack down on a chair and spinning to take in the artwork, the floral wallpaper, the homey and vintage vibe. "I like it."

"Lydia's husband cooks and Lyd makes the drinks. But watch her, she's got a heavy hand." He winks.

"Heard that!" Lydia calls out seconds before she appears, carrying a tray with two waters and two coffees.

I sit down at a table and Derek takes the chair across from me.

"You're right before the rush," Lydia informs us as she places our beverages down. "Hungry?"

Derek nods. "She can eat."

I grimace.

"Breakfast or dinner?" Lydia asks.

"I, um," I stammer.

"Don't think," the little grandma explains. "Just say whatever comes to mind first."

"Okay," I agree, wondering what kind of game we're playing.

"Breakfast or dessert?" she poses the next question.

"Breakfast," I respond.

"Sweet or savory?"

"Savory."

"Orange or green?"

"Green," I guess.

"Got it," Lydia says, nodding at me with approval in her eyes.

Did I make the right choices?

She glances at Derek. "I know what you're having," she informs him.

I sputter in laughter and Lydia gives me a cheeky grin. Then, she heads back to the kitchen. I take a sip of my coffee and cough, not expecting the sweet cream of Bailey's to coat my taste buds. "She spiked the coffee."

Derek grins. "Always. At least you got Bailey's. She definitely splashed brandy in mine."

I laugh, bewildered, but enjoying this strange experience. "Thanks for taking me here," I tell Derek sincerely.

"Sure," he brushes it off.

"Did you have fun today? At the lesson?" I was surprised when Dre said Derek would do the lessons. Until he entered the group home, I kept waiting for him to make an excuse and blow it off.

I haven't seen him much in the past few weeks and whatever weirdness or residual hurt I thought I'd feel today has eased by witnessing his music lesson.

Seeing him interact with the kids, especially Jem and Sarah, was different. I understood what Dre meant about Derek being loyal and having emotions and heart underneath his blasé attitude and untouchable swagger.

"It was interesting," he offers cryptically.

I laugh. "Come on, just admit it. You had more fun than you thought. Sarah is adorable and Jem is relatable. And you can't wait to come back next week."

The corner of his mouth twitches but his dark eyes remain serious. "Jem is relatable."

"He reminds you of a younger version of yourself," I guess.

Derek snorts and shakes his head. "At first, yeah. But Jem's all Dre. Sarah reminds me of me."

"Shut up," I say playfully. No way is sweet, eager Sarah anything like young Derek was.

"I'm serious," he says. "When I first met Dre, we had the same foster parents. Karen and Simon. Karen was nice, decent. She was a nurse and worked a lot of night shifts at the hospital. Simon—" He pauses and bites his lip.

I lean forward, hanging onto his words. It's the most Derek's ever confided in me about his past and I don't want to miss a word. I don't want to overlook one well-meaning glance or half smirk. My heart thuds in my temples and my stomach knots, painfully, as I know this story won't have a happily-ever-after.

"Simon was a smarmy motherfucker." Derek's eyes glint with untamed anger. "He looked the part. Dressed and spoke well. But behind closed doors he was a mean drunk. Used to smack Dre around. And Dre, he was a tough motherfucker. Had to be to survive. But Simon would make him cower."

Nausea rolls through me and swims in my stomach. I grip my coffee mug, feel my knuckles crack.

"I fucked up," Derek continues. He bites the corner of his mouth and shakes his head. His eyes cut to mine. Hold and bleed. "I fucked up."

I swipe my tongue along my bottom lip to wet it. My throat is dry, and my mouth feels parched, but I don't lift my coffee mug. "What happened?"

"I looked up to Dre. We were together for nearly a year and he was good to me. Took the beatings Simon meant for me. I was still young, like Sarah. I wanted to do something good for Dre, pay him back for his kindness. I thought if Simon didn't have liquor, he wouldn't be so mean. He was nice to Karen. He was even funny when he didn't drink. He was sober on the nights she didn't work. So, I drained his liquor cabinet. Emptied all the bottles."

"Oh, Derek," I sigh, knowing what's coming.

"Yeah," Derek agrees. "Dre got blamed. He took the beating of his fucking life. Ran away that night."

"Shit," I swear.

"He's seven years older than me."

"Really?" I blurt out.

Derek snickers. "Yeah. I know, he looks younger."

I shrug because it's the truth.

"Dre lived on the streets for the next two years or so. He was fucking homeless, Allegra. Doing whatever it took to survive. That's when Buck found him."

"Buck," I whisper, pieces clicking together in my mind.

"Buck got him on a good path. And my stupid fuckup nearly ruined his life," Derek concludes.

"It was an accident. You were just a kid," I point out. "You were trying to do something good. The right thing."

"The right thing," Derek scoffs. "I should've known better." He dismisses my words. "Deep down, I did know better. Maybe it was fucking denial. But after that, after I lost Dre, yeah, I stopped being Sarah." He smirks. "I started taking Simon's beatings. Every fucking night. He and Karen were on the rocks by then and living under their roof was pure hell. I started acting out, getting into fights, being a hothead."

"What changed?" I ask.

"Music," he explains. "My music teacher knew I had it rough and took me under his wing. Let me hang in the music room and fiddle on the guitars. I started staying after school to take lessons and when Mr. Robertson gifted me a guitar, everything changed. My world opened up. Music saved me."

"Wow," I murmur, viewing Derek through a new lens. Seeing the boy behind the man who endured years of hardship and loss and abuse to become a bona fide rockstar. "That's, your story is—"

"A disaster?"

"Incredible," I protest. "Hopeful." I sigh. "Uplifting."

Derek snickers. "You're too goddamn good, Allegra."

I shake my head. "Derek," I say slowly, wondering if I should ask the next question or let it go.

"Ask me," he states, correctly reading the hesitation in my tone.

I bite my bottom lip. "Did you ever know your mom and dad?"

He sighs and runs a hand through his hair. "Yeah. I knew my mom. She's an addict but I spent my childhood with her. Even spent some time at Maybelle's House." He grins to take the pain out of that statement.

My heart breaks and my stomach twists as I think of Derek as a little boy, huddling in the women's shelter the way I've witnessed other kids do. I clear my throat. "I had no idea."

He shrugs. "She left when I was seven. Never knew my dad except..."

"Except?"

He shakes his head. "I keep getting these emails from Jess that my father is trying to connect with me."

A rush of excitement runs through me and I try to tamp it down. "And?"

He chortles. "And nothing. I mean, the guy is doing it the right way, through a lawyer and all that. But I don't buy it. What? He found me now? Now that I'm worth millions." He scoffs. "Could all be bullshit. It most likely is."

"But aren't you curious?" I wonder.

He cracks his neck. "Curiosity killed the cat, Allegra," he teases.

"A cat's got nine lives, Derek."

He grins. Nods in agreement. But then he quips, "I've already used most of mine."

He says it teasingly, but I read the truth behind his tone. It sobers me and I drop my eyes. I can't imagine Derek's childhood and all he endured to get to this point.

When I look up, he's watching me closely.

"Don't feel bad for me, Stellina," he whispers. "I do just fine."

"I know," I reply.

"Your food is ready!" Lydia hollers.

Derek gives one final nod and the heaviness of our conversation eases as Lydia appears. She places a savory crepe filled with ham and cheese and mushrooms in front of me. It's plated on a sage green dish and I laugh.

"Oh, this looks delicious," I comment.

Lydia beams. "It is!"

Derek snorts and glances at his dish. Mac and cheese. He grins at Lydia. "Thanks, Lyd. Tell Henry thanks too."

"Of course. I've got a tin of chocolate chip cookies for you too." She pats his head like he's still a little boy. An enthusiastic, eager, open kid who didn't take beatings or carry around crushing guilt or search for survival in the chords of a guitar.

The realization makes the back of my nose burn and unshed tears pierce the corners of my eyes. Who would Derek be if he never lost Dre? Who would he have become if he remained a Sarah?

Lydia moves back toward the kitchen.

I lift my fork in the air, let it hover between Derek and me. "Truce?" I offer, thawing the remainder of our cold front.

He smirks and clanks his fork against mine. "Truce."

Should I tell him that I'm coming on tour? Should I gauge his reaction to having me traipse along Europe with him and the band?

I turn the idea over in my mind as we tuck into our food.

"Oh my God!" I moan appreciatively at how good my crepe is.

Cutting off a piece, I place it on Derek's plate. His eyes snap up to mine, surprise and something I can't read in their depths.

"You'll like it," I promise.

"Yeah," he agrees.

"You deserve good things, Derek," I tell him sincerely.

His mouth twists. "I have good things, Allegra. You see my life, it's what dreams are made of."

I open my mouth to press my point. To confide that Levi invited me on tour. To tell him *things*. But his phone buzzes, skittering over the top of the table.

Derek and I glance at it at the same time.

Jenn appears on the screen, and I swallow back my words, relieved I didn't say them yet.

Of course, he's seeing her. Screwing her. Maybe even dating her?

Derek's nostrils flare and he exhales noisily, reaching out to flip his phone screen facedown. He silences the call.

Tendrils of hurt, of disappointment, crawl through my chest and flare up into my throat. I take a long sip of my spiked coffee to wash them away.

"You still deserve good things," I repeat quietly.

His eyes darken, unfathomable pools of regret. Of guilt and shame. But in their centers, I spy a flicker of determination.

My heart rate jumps, and I grip my fork tighter.

"No," he replies, and my hope dies. "I don't deserve any of the things I truly want. Never have and never will."

I stare at Derek for a long beat and search for slivers of

the eager, enthusiastic, whole little boy he described. I'm met with his resistance, all anger and bitterness.

I shake my head and cut another piece of my crepe. I drop it onto his plate.

Partly as reluctant acknowledgement, partly as quiet resignation.

SIXTEEN
DEREK

We come back from the studio and order a bunch of takeout. We've been hitting our recording sessions hard this week and I'm simultaneously exhausted and restless. Drained and antsy. Desperate to kick back and stay in yet desiring a crowded pub and a cold beer.

"Fuck." I scrape my hand along my face, the sound of my palm grazing over my stubble loud in my eardrums.

Next to me, Mav shrugs. "I thought today went well."

"Wasn't terrible," Jameson agrees, opening the Styrofoam containers and arranging them on the kitchen island. "Nice call on jalapeño poppers."

"Right?" Levi says, swiping a popper and tossing it into his mouth.

I narrow my eyes at him, mentally counting down from five, before his face turns red and he starts to cough, spit dotting his shirtsleeve when he raises his wrist in front of his mouth. "Fucking amateur."

Mav passes Levi a beer.

Levi clears his throat and shakes his head, opting for a nacho instead of another popper. "A working tonight?"

It's pathetic that he directs his question to Mav. Levi is one of my best friends. We've been through a lot together, started out at the same time, in the same circuit, and rose through the ranks before teaming up to kick off The Burnt Clovers. He's like a brother to me, different from Dre, and I trust him.

But fuck if I don't like the way he treats his sister. He doesn't look out for Allegra the way he should; from where I'm sitting, he never has.

Mav checks his watch. "She was. She finished around five."

"It's nine," I point out.

Mav snorts. "Exactly." He shakes his head. "She probably went out with some friends."

"The Hawks girls," Levi agrees, nodding.

"Don't you think you should message her?" I ask Levi. "You know, check in."

"Why're you so worried about A all the time?" he counters.

"Why aren't you?" I spit back.

Mav points at me. "He's got a point," he tells Levi. "She's a Boston newb, who spends her days in a rough part of town and her nights with a professional hockey team." I sneer at the mention of the Hawks and Mav grins. "You should make up and play nice with Easton and Austin. They're good guys."

"We're not in a fight," I mutter before swearing. I fucking hate playing Mav's stupid childish games.

But he just beams at me like the little nuisance he is.

Jameson chuckles and pops the top on a beer, passing me the bottle. "Take the edge off, man."

I take a deep pull. The bitterness of the hops does absolutely nothing to redirect my thoughts. Who is

Allegra out with tonight? Where is she and what is she doing?

I saw her this morning during my music lesson with the kids and she didn't mention she had plans tonight. She didn't mention anything although she stayed the entire time and participated in the lesson.

My frustration soars. Since I confided my shit in her, I can't get a read on her. When she looks at me, it's not with anger or hurt, but acceptance. A few times, we kicked back to watch a movie together. One night, while watching a drama, our hands inched closer underneath the blanket. My pinky grazed hers and she pulled in an inhale, her eyes darting to mine. I linked my pinky and ring fingers over hers and squeezed, half holding her hand.

"What are you doing?" she murmured, a blush washing over her cheeks.

"Watching a movie," I replied.

She gave me half a smirk. "Why are you touching me?"

"Because," I sighed, then gave her the truth. "Because I can't *not* when you're sitting this close."

She studied me for a long beat. Then, she shifted closer, until our thighs pressed up against each other's. Allegra flipped her hand, palm up, and allowed me to lace our fingers together. I shifted our joined hands into her lap, and we sat like that, holding hands, with her head resting against my shoulder, for the remainder of the film.

It was simple and easy. Innocent and genuine. It was unlike anything I've ever experienced, and I wish it didn't make me crave more. Not just Allegra's mouth and curves but her thoughts and hopes. Her reasoning and her chatter. I want to know more about her friends and her life in LA, about her goals and her plans for after this summer.

Twice in the week that followed our exchange, I peeked

in on her while she slept, just to hear her even breathing. Just to check that she's okay. I prepared her coffee in the French press on the mornings she ran late. I looked for her poetry book or her headphones on the kitchen island when I walked through the front door. I like seeing little pieces of Allegra, of her life, in the brownstone, as part of my space.

But her schedule is busy and while she's always friendly toward me, that passivity remains. It's as if she's embraced our truce. She's okay with the budding friendship between us. She's okay that it's not more than that. Maybe she doesn't need me the way I'm starting to need, want, her. As a more permanent fixture in my life. As a relationship deeper than a fleeting connection or a temporary acquaintance.

It's messing with my head, how much I care for her. How normal we can act around each other, even with the longing that roots in my gut and the confusion that swirls in my mind. A type of understanding has emerged between us and although it should reassure me, her acknowledging my limitations, it doesn't.

Instead, I want her to push me to be better. To be more.

It's sadistic because I'll never rise to the challenge and yet...part of me wants to try.

My fingertips drum along the butcher block and I drain the beer. My eyelids feel heavy, my body slow. Fuck, I'm tired.

But my mind races.

It always does during songwriting. When I'm focused, I'm locked in. But now that recording is done for the day, my mind has turned to Allegra, and I hate that she's at the forefront of every thought.

I hate that I worry about her, wonder about her, as much as I do.

I move toward the refrigerator to grab a second beer when Levi's phone beeps.

He glances at the screen, his eyebrows pulling low as a sneer curls his lips.

"Fuck," he sighs.

"What?" I snap.

"Cyn and my sister." He waves his phone.

"She's out with Cynthia?" I growl, incredulous. Cynthia's a fun girl but as far as friends go, she's a shitty one. Look up an antonym for *loyal* and you'll find an image of Cynthia.

Mav grabs Levi's phone and chuckles at the photo on screen. His thumb swipes over the screen and he gives an impressed nod. "Okay, A. I see you, girl."

"Give me it." I grab the phone from him.

My growing annoyance flares into full-blown anger as I stare at the image on screen.

Allegra's perched on the knee of some dude I don't recognize—a Hawks player? Worse, a fucking random?—laughing at whatever dumb fuck thing he's saying. He's got his arm banded around her waist, and his other palm splayed on her upper thigh.

He's *touching* her like he wants her. Like he knows her. Like she's his.

"Fuck this," I murmur, tossing down Levi's phone.

Mav snatches it up. "But you missed the cute selfie of A and Cyn being—"

"Let's go," I bark at Levi.

"Cyn will have her doing body shots within the hour," Levi agrees, looking worried for the first time in weeks.

Is he high all the time now? Does he remember what it's like to be a sober, rational, caring big brother? Or friend?

Mav chuckles again as Jameson looks on, grinning.

"Good luck." Jameson lifts a beer in farewell.

"Yeah, we'll try not to polish this off." Mav gestures to the takeout containers.

"Whatever." I shake my head, shoving my feet into sandals by the front door.

Levi exchanges some words with Drew and Alfred and then, we're off.

"They're at Taps?" Alfred meets my gaze in the rearview mirror.

"Yeah," I mutter, recalling the well-worn interior of the bar from the photo.

"Cynthia's gotta cut this shit out," Levi murmurs beside me.

I turn and give him an incredulous look. "Seriously? You're more upset about Cynthia than your sister?"

He looks chagrined and turns away. "No, I'm furious with A, but Cyn..."

"What?"

"She pulls this shit to piss me off." His words are quiet.

Understanding dawns and I close my eyes, tapping the back of my head against the headrest. "You fucked Cynthia? Jesus, Levi, what's wrong with you?"

"Every now and then." His tone is harder now. Defensive.

"You're a shitty brother."

"What?" He shoves me in the ribs, and I open my eyes.

Glaring right at my best friend, I repeat, "You're a shitty brother. And Cynthia's a shitty friend."

Levi stares at me, hard eyes and an expressionless face. A mask. "We usually just screw when we're high."

I squint back. When has he gotten so good at shutting his shit down? "Levi, don't you see how manipulative and messed up Cynthia is? Hell, she hooked up with the guy

Allegra crushed on at Allegra's seventeenth birthday party!"

Levi squints at me like he's having a hard time keeping up with our conversation.

"That's messed up, man. That's breaking girl code or whatever the hell it is. And then, you get with her? That's breaking sibling code! I don't even have a sibling and I know that. Jesus." I shove Levi for good measure. "Allegra deserves better than your bullshit."

He sighs and scrubs his hands over his eyes. "Allegra and Cyn go way back; you're overreacting. We only screw when we're lit anyway, man. Doesn't mean jack shit."

I shake my head at him, disgusted. Why the hell does Allegra keep trying so hard for his approval, for his affection, when he would go and get with a girl who repeatedly hurt her in high school?

When I met Levi, years ago, he was the life of the party. The charismatic, fun, engaging guy that could charm a grandma as easily as a toddler. Everyone wanted a piece of him, everyone wanted some of his energy. His light.

And now...

"So, what? You're lit all the time now?" I ask, wondering if he's ever straight.

He shrugs, not bothering to respond.

I'd push the issue farther, especially if his shit is going to mess with the band, but Alfred announces our arrival.

Drew gets out first and does a quick sweep before opening the door for Levi and me. We're hustled through a side entrance, and I remind myself to stay cool. Level-headed.

I'm not here to make a scene.

I'm not here to make trouble.

I'm just here to get Allegra home safely.

But then I see her, half splayed out on top of the goddamn bar. Her tank top is hiked up her smooth torso, a man's hand on her thigh, holding her in place. Keeping her pinned to the bar as she half sits up, resting on her elbow.

Her long hair spills over her shoulder and if it was any other woman, I'd stop to admire how gorgeous she is. Like a mermaid. Flawless and ethereal.

But it's Allegra so I rush the fucker and snatch his hand off her body. "Get lost."

"Hey!" He spins but when he sees my face, notes my hand, with my middle and ring fingernails polished a dark navy, he swears.

Shaking off my hold, he raises both hands in the air. "Didn't know she was yours, Reign."

"Get. Lost," I repeat through clenched teeth. My body buzzes with fury and adrenaline rushes through my veins. Concern churns my stomach raw, and anger—unfiltered and desperate—builds in my limbs. I want to knock this guy out for the sheer thrill of knocking someone out.

My vision slants on the edges and I blink to clear it. I haven't reacted like this in a long time but right now, I want to unleash all the pent-up shit I've been trying to squash. Suddenly, it has nowhere to go but out.

"Shit," another patron mutters, correctly reading my reaction.

I drag in an inhale, feeling my nostrils flare.

"Derek," Allegra's voice is low. Confused.

I look at her and a swell of emotion counteracts my anger. She's the fucking poison and antidote all in one. God, she's gorgeous. Looking up at me with big, brown eyes and a curious expression. Doesn't she get it?

Doesn't she see how much she messes with me? How much power she wields?

In my peripheral vision, I watch as cell phones are surreptitiously unveiled, their cameras pointed in my direction.

Fucking vultures.

"This is low, even for you," Levi murmurs to Cynthia, shaking her shoulder. But his words lack the depth of disappointment to make them meaningful.

She laughs softly, beaming at him. Her blue eyes are wide and blown. "You came, didn't you?"

Christ. I pinch the bridge of my nose. Does Allegra even know her friend is higher than a fucking satellite orbiting Mars right now?

"Derek," Allegra murmurs again. She's peering at me in confusion. She moves slowly and I realize she's three sheets to the wind.

Her palm slips on the slick bar top, and she stumbles forward. As she begins to pitch over the side of the bar, I step to her, keeping her upright. I cup the back of her head, cradle her to my chest, and lower my mouth to her ear. With her in my arms, some of my anger recedes. Her well-being takes center stage and I grip onto that.

As much as I want to demand answers and shake some damn sense into her, I don't want to end up plastered all over gossip rags and trending as a chyron on the bottom of television screens.

"We're leaving now. Pull your shirt down, climb off the bar, and follow me out the back door. Got it?" I thread my fingers through her hair and give a little tug to ensure she hears me.

Dark eyes find mine, glinting in anger.

I grin. As her fury increases, mine deflates. She's with me; I've got her.

A few ballsy cell phones move closer.

In her peripheral vision, Allegra must note them because she dips her head and tugs down her tank top.

"I'm gonna get her home," Levi says, holding up a sloppy, but beaming, Cynthia. She's seriously pathetic.

And my best friend is a loser for chasing her.

But Levi leaving plays in my interest so I nod. "Go with Alfred and Drew. I'll text Samson. I got Allegra; I'll get her home."

"Thanks, man." Levi glances at his sister. "We'll be talking tomorrow, A. This shit won't fly in the fall."

She snorts, either in acceptance or refusal, I have no idea. And what the hell does Levi mean, "in the fall"?

Allegra starts to slip again and my attention snaps back to her.

I wait until Levi and Cynthia leave Taps before I glower at the beauty before me. "Ready?"

She slides off the bar ledge and I settle her and Cynthia's tab. Then, I grip her hand in mine and drag her through the back entrance, into the humid night.

I turn toward her, my mouth open, ready to unleash my line of questioning. Allegra stops and pivots toward me, her eyes blazing, her expression enraged. Her presence expands as her eyes fly across my frame, scanning me from head to toe with pure disdain that infuriates me. And fucking turns me on.

She flings her arms to the side, the thin strap of her tank top slipping off her shoulder. Her hair is wavy, the front pieces curling to frame her face, and I want to fist it, tug hard, and take the angry slash of her mouth.

Before I can suggest as much, her arm darts out and her palm connects with my cheek. My neck swivels and my face stings as I reel back, clasping the side of my head.

Holy shit. Allegra just slapped me. I rub at the pain in

my cheek and cock my head, waiting for her words. She's so angry, she smolders. It's the sexiest she's ever looked, and I take a moment to appreciate her beauty. Her ferocity. Her sheer power.

"What the fuck is wrong with you?" Allegra bellows, glaring at me.

I can't stop the smile from forming as I watch in fascination as my little star begins to burn.

Fuck, she is magnificent.

SEVENTEEN
ALLEGRA

My skin is too tight, too containing, for the hot fury coursing through my veins. I vibrate with rage. Years of pent-up hurts, old wounds, accusations, threaten to hurl from my mouth with deadly precision.

Right now, Derek is my most suitable and only target. He's staring at me, grinning, when I want to rip his face off.

My palm burns from where I slapped him. The crack of my hand connecting with his face echoes in the sticky air.

I curl my fingers into a fist, clasping my hand against my chest, as shock rocks through me.

Oh gosh, I hit someone.

I slapped Derek.

Little tendrils of panic begin to coil and loosen in my limbs. My mind races.

His eyes hold a glint of satisfaction I can't stand.

"What the fuck is wrong with you?" I repeat, quieter this time.

Derek's head turns a fraction, his gaze landing on the brick wall at my back. I watch the emotions he usually keeps locked down ripple across his face.

Anger, pride, fascination.

Heat, desire, want.

My other hand curls into a fist. The tipsy buzz I had going on is obliterated. Instead, I feel wild. Hot and needy and daring. Angry and frantic and reckless.

"Why the hell did you come?" I question Derek. "You have Jenn. You have every fucking woman in this damn city." My hands spring open and I press them against Derek's chest, shoving him.

He shuffles back half a step, one of his hands grabbing mine, trapping it against his beating heart. His grin widens.

"Can't I have some fun?" I continue. "Can't I meet a man who makes me feel things?"

His humor evaporates. That taunting smile flattens into a thin line. A razor's edge. His nostrils flare.

"What things?" he demands, his voice laced with arsenic.

I laugh but it's not funny. No, the sound that cuts the air is half bellowing, half delirious. Desperate.

Things that make me forget you! I want to hurl the words at him, but they're too telling. They give too much away.

Instead, I glare at him, my chest heaving, my fingernails scraping against the thin fabric of his T-shirt. I want to claw at him. Wail against his larger-than-life demeanor that keeps me pinned in place.

Pining and hoping and dreaming.

I work a swallow, my throat dry, my eyes clear. "Whole," I spit the word.

Watch as it lands. His carefully controlled expression cracks for a heartbeat.

His face crumples, his shoulders sag, and he swears.

"Fucking hell, Stellina." My nickname is a plea on his lips. A curse and a wish and a prayer.

Derek's neck snaps up. His eyes find mine and pierce me to the core. They're blacker than midnight, edged in steel. His mouth twists, a snarl. He pushes into me, keeping my fingers trapped in his, like a vise, as he backs us against the brick wall.

My bare shoulders cut into the hard surface, and it scrapes against my back. I straighten my shoulders, narrowing my eyes at Derek as he lines his body up against mine.

"What are you doing?" I ask. But my bravado has slipped. Nerves skate down my arms and zip up my stomach. I tug my hand, but his fingers tighten their hold. "What do you want from me?"

He snorts, his upper lip curling. But his eyes don't leave mine. He doesn't even blink.

The air around us is oppressive. Bearing down with a relentless heat that steals the oxygen from my lungs. Beads of perspiration roll down my spine, pool in the small of my back. My hands feel clammy.

Heat gathers between my thighs. Achy and throbbing. A slice of well-meaning fear that morphs into angst when Derek lowers his mouth to the shell of my ear.

He breathes out and his breath skates over my neck. I shiver and feel his arousal, long and thick and painfully hard, grind against my abdomen.

"Everything," he murmurs one word. He rolls his hips, grinding against me again. Making his desire clear. His intention known. "Every fucking thing, Stellina."

I suck in a shallow breath, try to clear my thoughts. Gain control over this situation.

Derek turns his face, the tip of his nose tracing a line

along my cheek. Then, his mouth is on mine and all rational thoughts disappear.

I hover between detonating and melting for him. My body falls slack, a puppet in his hands. Derek becomes my master, coaxing and demanding and controlling every aspect of this encounter.

His lips are hard against mine, his tongue plundering as it invades my mouth. He kisses me brashly and I buck against him, pressing my chest into his and arching my neck to meet him. Kiss for kiss. Nip for nip. Lick for lick.

He looms over me, dark and dangerous, blotting out the light. Stealing my breath. His hands find mine, lacing our fingers together and bringing our joined hands over my head. My knuckles slam into the bricks and I roll my hips, feeling his length.

"Give it to me then," I order, my voice harsh.

"Fuck!" he swears, pulling back to glare at me. "You have no fucking clue what you want. What you're asking me."

I shake my head. "Don't patronize me, Derek. You think you're the first man I've been with? The first guy to touch—"

He growls and drops my hand. Backs up a few steps.

My chest heaves as I watch him, wondering what he'll do next. God, I'm half out of my mind with lust. With a desperate desire that threatens to consume me. Worse, I want it to.

I want him to—what? Take me against a wall in a back alley?

It's depraved. It's against everything I've been taught my entire life. It's immoral and wrong and filthy.

But my pussy clenches and throbs. My nipples are hard,

poking into the rough material of my bra. Everything feels swollen and heavy and tight.

My mind buzzes, a whirring sound filling my ears that distorts reality. My fingers tremble, responding to my body's desire. They skate across my denim shorts. Slide over my hip and down my thigh, toward my core. Derek watches in rapt fascination, his breathing heavy, his nostrils flaring.

I hold his gaze, bold and daring and furious.

The pad of my index finger meets the seam of my thigh. My back arches imperceptibly. I'm desperate for touch. For release. I swipe one finger over the seam that runs between my thighs and buck against the gentle contact.

Before I can do it again, Derek's between my legs. His hand swats mine away and he hikes me up against the wall. One hand under my ass, supporting my weight, the other tight on my ribs.

"Hook your leg around me," he commands.

I do, pressing my back into the wall.

"You're pure perfection, Allegra," he says, using his weight to pin me in place.

One hand makes quick work of the button and zipper on my jean shorts. Then, his tongue is in my mouth, his hand is in my pants, and I'm hovering in the air. Rocked between his skillful touch and a brick wall.

It's delicious.

I give him my body weight and let my eyes close. Sensations rock through me as Derek kisses me with abandon. Our tongues twist, dueling, for command. But he quickly overpowers mine as his fingers slip through the wet folds of my pussy.

I'm so wet for him, the sound of my arousal explodes in my eardrums. Blots out the buzzing and sings like a chorus, inching me higher with every octave.

"Oh God," I murmur.

"Fuck, baby." Derek's mouth is by my ear again. He drags two fingers against my core. "Dripping for me."

"Ung," I make a nonsensical sound, turned on by his words. Turned on by my reaction to him. Turned on by how wrong this is, out in the public where anyone can see us. See me writhing, dragging my head back and forth against the hard brick, and mewling for more. It's shameless. Forbidden. And so damn delicious.

"This what you want?" His finger teases against my entrance. My hips rock on their own accord and he snickers. "Yeah, my baby needs this, right?"

"Uh-huh." *My baby.* Am I his?

He presses one finger into me, so slowly, I cry out.

Then, he adds a second and slides them inside. Withdraws. Back in again.

"Derek," I pant.

"That's it. Say my name, Stellina."

"Derek," I manage again.

He fucks me with his fingers and the friction is wonderful. A burn gathers in my core, spreading into an exquisite heat. It grows, expands, takes over, as I vibrate in Derek's arms.

"Tell me what you want, Allegra." His voice is gruff. His control is slipping and mine is nonexistent.

"Everything," I breathe out. My head rolls against the wall. I force my eyes open and find his. He watches me with intent, his expression tighter than I've ever seen it.

Naked desire pools in his irises and he's breathing hard, panting in unison with me.

"Everything, Derek," I repeat his words.

He presses his thumb against my clit, a gentle whisper.

Pushes his fingers deep inside my pussy and curls them. Then, his thumb circles my clit once, twice and—

"Oh God. I'm coming," I tell him, my fingers clenching at his shoulders. I break apart in his arms. A tidal wave of sensation, of messy, complicated, fucked-up feelings and delicious, delightful, desperate warmth rushing through my body.

Derek holds me, watching me with pure fascination, as I shatter. Pieces of me—shards and slivers and sentiments—slam back into place, but they're rearranged. I'm half disoriented, half enchanted.

"Oh God," I whisper.

Derek's hand squeezes my ass as he gently lowers me to my feet.

I sag against the wall, needing its sturdiness to keep me upright as my legs threaten to give out.

My denim shorts are unbuttoned, hanging off one hip, but I don't bother fixing them. Instead, my fingers splay against the wall at my back and I try to regulate my breathing, to make sense of what just happened.

Derek keeps his eyes trained on me, his lids hooded with desire. I watch him through drugged eyes.

He pops his fingers into his mouth, sucking them clean. He pulls them out quickly, a string of saliva mixed with my arousal stretching from his lips to his fingertips. He smears it against my mouth before slamming his palm against the wall above my head.

Derek dips down and I raise my gaze. He catches my eyes and, keeping them open, drags his mouth over mine.

"I'm the man who makes you feel things," he reminds me in a low, threatening voice. "No one else."

My knees shake, my heart rate erratic.

"Now button your jeans. Samson's on his way and I told your brother I'd get you home."

"You did," I retort, surprising us both with my vulgarity. Honesty.

Derek narrows his eyes as he drinks in my face. His gaze tracks my expression, as if committing it to memory. "You're too big for this, Stellina."

I shake my head, not wanting to hear these words. Again.

"Push too hard and you'll burn right the fuck out," he warns. Then, he palms my hips, squeezing once, before he straightens my shorts and zips them up.

"Let's go." He turns, walking a few steps ahead of me.

I watch him go, note the strength in his shoulders, the casual gait of his walk.

But I know I affect him. Derek Reiner can have any woman in Boston, but deep down, he wants me.

Will he take me down dark, winding alleys in London? Against ancient ruins in Rome?

Swiping the back of my hand over my mouth, I laugh.

He wants me.

EIGHTEEN
DEREK

The sound of Allegra's moans explode behind my eyelids. The desperation in her touch swims through my veins. Her scent, vanilla and needy, sweet and sexy, burns my nostrils as I greedily inhale.

Give it to me then.

A taunting smirk. Knowing eyes.

A too-big heart. Caring touch.

Her heat on my fingertips, her tongue in my mouth, her panting cry when she—

Fuck. I sit straight up in bed. My sheets are twisted around my legs and the black wife beater I crashed in sticks to my chest, damp with sweat. And longing.

I pluck the material away, tugging on it a few times to create a breeze against my heated skin. My head is too heavy; my mind whirling.

Allegra Rousell is invading my every thought. Even in sleep.

I dig the heels of my hands into my eyes and scrub. It does shit to wash away the image of her, keyed up and shattering, pinned between my body and that filthy alley wall.

But fuck if she wasn't my undoing.

How the hell am I supposed to move past that night? Our exchange.

Now that I know her taste, have swallowed her want and coated my throat in her need, I'm screwed.

It's been three days since I ground my cock against Allegra's abdomen, shoved my hand down her shorts, and brought her to climax.

Three nights of night terrors that are as beautiful as they're dreadful.

She's too young. Too good.

Levi's my best friend. My bandmate.

I'll ruin her, destroy that vulnerability I've tried to protect.

I'm not boyfriend material. I don't do monogamous. I'm incapable of commitment.

I will fucking shred her.

But now that I've kissed her, I can't stop.

Two days ago, I dragged my fingertips across the small of her back when I passed her in the kitchen. Heard her shaky inhale, felt the shiver of anticipation that danced through her body. Yesterday, she caught me off guard, stepping into the hallway from her shower wrapped in a towel.

A bright white, too short towel, that slipped just enough to give me a glimpse of a dusty pink nipple and a perfect teardrop tit. A delectable handful I'd like to test the weight of. One I'd like to pull into my mouth and suck on.

When she caught me staring, she bit her bottom lip, and I swore. Turned right around and slammed my bedroom door. Jerked off to the thought of spraying my cum all over her titties, her wet hair a curtain down her back.

I am an awful friend. A terrible bandmate.

A depraved man who wants the woman I can't have.

Stellina.

Still, the torture continues.

Now that she's gotten a taste, she's jonesing as hard as I am. And so, we've started a new chapter. A dangerous dance. A game where neither of us will win.

There are no victors in deception. And that's exactly what Allegra and I are doing. We're deceiving everyone around us.

Worst of all, we're lying to ourselves.

"DAMN, I don't know how A wakes up so early," Mav comments the following morning. He bites into a Pop-Tart, licking a smudge of strawberry filling from the side of his mouth.

"She really likes working at the group home. Loves the kids," Levi agrees.

"Yeah," Mav laughs. "She's become Dre's right hand. Not to mention, she's basically Buck's sidekick at the soup kitchen."

I make an espresso. Even though I fell back to sleep last night, the hours weren't restful. I'm exhausted and by the frustration already flaring in my stomach, it's going to be a long day.

"Claire really took A under her wing too." Levi drains his coffee and places his mug down, keeping his fingers tucked around the handle. "It's good for Allegra, to have some friends here that are hers." He shakes his head. "Takes the pressure off me, you know? I don't want to be entertaining my little sister all the damn time." He cuts his eyes to me. "Thanks again for getting her home the other night."

I shrug, letting the bitter coffee wash away the guilt that

churns my stomach. If only Levi knew I got his sister off in the alley that cuts behind Taps. If only he knew that I reveled in watching her fall apart. It was a natural high, seeing Allegra break under my touch. Watching the color in her cheeks bloom. Witness the relief in her naked gaze.

Levi would kill me on principle, and I'd deserve it. I take another sip of my espresso.

Mav gives me a strange look. At his watchful gaze, I lift an eyebrow.

He shrugs and turns his attention back to Levi. "Can't believe you're fucking Cynthia."

"Fucked," Levi corrects. "It's not a continual thing." He pauses. "I mean, it's usually when we're high so…"

"You're fucked up," Mav tells him straight. He shakes his head in disappointment. "Your sister deserves more."

Levi groans. "Now you sound like Derek."

Mav arches his eyebrows and cuts me a look. I shrug.

"Pay attention, Levi, before you get in too deep. That girl's a mess," he warns. Then, he shrugs again. "Not that I should talk." He polishes off his Pop-Tart. "We hitting the studio later?"

"Yeah. We gotta stay on track," I remind them of the album we haven't completed. "Then I'm doing a music lesson at the group house."

"Sweet. Then, out?" Levi asks.

Mav shrugs. "Flip's having a thing."

I don't say anything. If the guys head out and get trashed at Flip's, the house will be empty. Save for Allegra. And me.

A buzz of anticipation rolls through my limbs. Excitement.

I haven't felt this way in a long time.

It's the same expectation that fills me before a show.

Gathering low in my gut, intensifying, and surging forward when I step onto a stage, a guitar slung over my shoulder, the roar of a crowd at my feet.

It's adrenaline and desperation, heady and overpowering.

It's the thrill of the moment, the excitement of knowing.

It's the salvation I seek and the fact that time alone with Allegra inspires it, feels like a dangerous gift. A bad omen and a sweet promise rolled together.

"You in?" Mav lifts his chin in my direction. He's got that strange look in his eyes again, like he sees through me.

I force myself to straighten. Stay calm. I'm psyching myself out. Mav's not a damn mind reader. He sees exactly what I want him to see.

I could beg off. Make up an excuse. I could pretend I've got plans lined up with Dre.

"Maybe we can rope Jameson in too." Levi rubs his hands together.

Allegra's eyes, darkened with desire, ringed with hope, flash through my mind.

No, if I stay, I'll cross the only line left between us. I'll obliterate it in my haste to take her. Taste her. Feel her.

Claim her.

And there will be no coming back from that. No sweet salvation or forbidden touches. No secret glances or stolen kisses.

Only heartache and hurt. Pain and punishment.

Our chapter will close, our dance will conclude, our game will end. By forfeit.

And I'm not ready to let it—her—go.

I clear my throat. "Sure, whatever. I'm in."

Mav claps his hands, surprised but happy with my response.

Levi's phone beeps and my friend grins. "Jameson's in too."

"All right," Mav cheers. "Tonight will be like old times. The four of us out together; it's gonna be epic."

"Yeah," I say, even though my heart isn't in it.

But I go through the motions. I do all the shit I've gotta get done for the day. I hit the studio and conduct a music lesson for the kids. Allegra skips it, working at the soup kitchen with Buck instead, and I try not to let my disappointment show even though Dre knows I'm off.

I note that Allegra posts to her social media twice. A selfie of her and Buck making silly faces and a photo of a large group of people toasting together, shouting out the soup kitchen.

Both are sincere and playful. Both are representative of Allegra.

I can't mess with the genuine vibe she gives off.

So I dress in a designer shirt and black jeans. I touch up the navy polish on my fingernails. Delete another email from my so-called father who can't take a hint. Then, I slip my wallet and phone into my back pocket.

We head to Flip's house. My bandmates are keyed up and I force myself to join in. To commit to having a good time.

Mav kicks it off with a round of tequila shots and I try not to think of the last time I took one. The way my fingertips grazed Allegra's lips when I held up a slice of lime.

We take a photo. The four of us are joking around, shot glasses and red Solo cups littering the kitchen island in front of us. Levi blows a smoke ring, and the drifting smoke infiltrates one side of the photo, giving it a hazy, grainy look.

Grinning, I post it to my official social media.

Caption: *Good choices with the boys. (Whiskey glass emoji)*

I know Allegra will see the photo. I know it will pull her up short and make her wonder what I'm up to tonight the same way it does to me when I search her socials and analyze her posts.

It's thrilling, to know she'll be thinking of me.

I laugh and take another shot. Do a line of coke when it's offered. Accept a pill when it's pressed in my hand.

The night is a rager. Time passes in flashes of lights and snippets of sound. In slow motion snapshots and faded recollections.

Sweat beads on my forehead. My palms tingle. A woman's hair, dark and luscious, wraps around my fist. Moans and pants. Clumsy hands and desperate mouths.

I wake up hours later, sprawled in the center of a bed. A brunette is on my right, a blonde on my left. A purple lace thong is clutched in my hand.

"Fuck," I mutter, staring at the coffered ceiling. I blink a few times to clear my vision, chase away the dryness that hugs my eyes.

I lift my head a few inches and drop it back against the pillow. My head is heavy, my body weightless. Am I still fucked up?

Probably.

I turn on my side and let my eyes close.

Allegra's laughter fills my mind and I screw my eyes tighter, pushing it—her—away.

She doesn't belong here, in my depraved reality.

She never has.

The brunette nuzzles closer, and I let her, momentarily pretending she's a different brunette. One who isn't nameless and wasted.

One who makes my heart race and my soul hope.

One who would hate my fucking guts if she could see me now.

I snake my hand under the pillow, pulling back when it collides with my phone.

Snorting, I angle the phone and snap a photo. It's mostly my naked upper body and my twisted smirk, lifeless eyes. Strands of long brown hair and a shock of blonde waves are in both corners, the rumpled bed sheets evident.

You still deserve good things. Her voice rings in my ear.

No, I don't. I never have. I never will.

Knowing it's for Allegra's own good and my fucking sanity, I post the photo.

Caption: *Better decisions with the girls.* (*Rock on hand emoji*)

Then, I roll over and fall back to sleep.

NINETEEN
ALLEGRA

The pain that cuts through my chest is enough to make me double over.

I drop my phone, watching as it clatters to the floor. I don't move to catch it. I can't.

Because my vision swims and my windpipe constricts, and the back of my nose stings.

The house is quiet this morning. Empty.

None of the guys came home last night. Other than a text from Mav that read *don't wait up*, none of them even contacted me.

Witnessing Derek's story, him in bed with two women, messy sheets, and a crooked smile, devastates me.

I sink to the floor and drop the back of my head against the bathroom door.

What kind of guy coaxes a woman's body into pleasure—immense, overwhelming, out-of-this-world pleasure—and then screws two randoms in a stranger's bed?

My eyes close and tears leak out, sliding down my cheeks. They move slowly at first but as more images explode in my mind—Derek and the blonde, Derek and the brunette, Derek and the blonde and the brunette—they fall faster.

Soon, I'm sobbing into my open palms, hunched over my knees. The backs of my hands rub against bare knees and my denim shorts ride up my ass. I don't move to fix them. Discomfort has nothing on the heartache I feel.

I don't know how long I sit on the bathroom floor but eventually, a chime on my phone forces me to move.

I pick up my phone, breathe a sigh of relief that the screen isn't cracked, and almost smile when I read Kenny's name in our group chat.

Kenny: We miss you, A! Senior year is gonna be shit without you.

Kenny: (Image: Ivy, Nova, and Mckenna posing on the beach)

Ivy: See, Mckenna came around!

Nova: We'll see you in Barcelona, baby!

I instantly heart the picture and message back.

Me: Maybe I'll be back...

Ivy: Uh-oh...

Kenny: What's wrong?

Me: Why are you all up?

Nova: Gross sunrise runs, remember? Kenny is a tyrant.

Ivy: She's killing us, Allegra.

Kenny: They'll thank me when they're stronger. What's going on?

Nova: You don't send us any good stories...

Kenny: That's Nova not-so-subtly begging for some tea.

Nova: (praying hands emoji)

Me: Nothing good to share... None of the guys came home last night.

Nova: And Reign posted a picture...

Me: You saw it?

Nova: Sorry! Can't help it. Now that I know YOU KISSED HIM, I've become obsessed.

Me: I was 17!

Ivy: Still counts.

Kenny: Totally counts.

Me: I gotta get to the soup kitchen. Fill you girls in later?

Ivy: Fill us in on...? Are you coming back? Or did something happen with Reign?

Kenny: Are you still planning to go to Europe and work things out with Levi?

Nova: Please tell me something happened with Reign! (three fire emojis) I need something to have happened with Reign!

Ivy: Nova is living through you.

Nova: I am. I'm not even trying to hide it.

Kenny: Are you okay, Allegra?

Me: Yeah, just, weird morning... Gotta get to work. Talk later.

Kenny: We miss you!

Ivy: And love you.

Nova: Always. Call us, bitch.

I send a thumbs-up emoji and end the chat. Then, I drag myself from the floor. I wash my face and fix my hair. I go through the motions, trying to stitch up the mess that's bleeding out in the cavity of my chest.

Derek doesn't regularly post on social media. So why would he randomly post him and two women, in bed, the morning after?

Is he trying to get my attention?

Hurt my feelings? Or pride?

Warn me away?

Derek kisses me like he wants me, like he can't stand the thought of not having me. So for him to do this...

There must be a reason. An explanation.

And I want to know what the hell it is.

I SPEND all morning and afternoon at the soup kitchen, working with Buck. At first, my pal gives me space, knowing it's an early morning. Buck's witnessed me hungover a time or two this summer. He usually chuckles or cracks a joke. Once, he brought me a Hair of the Dog from the pub across the street, promising it would cure me.

It did.

But as the day drags on and my demeanor doesn't soften, my friend knows something is up.

I can't climb out of the rut I laid down in this morning. My head is tangled up on Derek and what he did, and didn't, do last night. My heart feels cracked, my body numb. Half of me wants to sob, the other half wants to rage.

If I think about it too long, imagining his mouth on her skin, his hands tangled in her hair, his kiss on her lips, my fingers tremble.

Twice, I dropped trays I was carrying.

Once, a woman had to repeat her order three times before I processed her words.

Still, I hope Buck will let it slide. At the end of the day, when we've cleaned everything up and all is ready and prepped for the following morning, Buck lifts both eyebrows. "You ready to talk yet?"

I glance up and manage a smile.

Buck leans against the broom handle, his hand wrapped around its center, his dark eyes steady on mine.

Wisdom wrinkles his face and knowing shimmers in his gaze.

"I'm fine, Buck." I wave a hand.

"What's his name, A?" he asks, not unkindly.

I sigh, letting my shoulders slump. "That obvious, huh?"

"That obvious," Buck confirms.

I roll my lips together, wondering how much to divulge. What do I even say? Derek and I are...nothing. Hell, no one knows our history. No one else knows anything. Is Buck, a Bostonian who is boys with Dre, going to be the guy I confide in?

"You hungry?" he asks.

I shake my head. I have no appetite.

"Too bad." He clucks his tongue. "I'm taking you for a burger."

"A burger?"

"And a milkshake," Buck confirms, placing the broom in the closet. "Come on."

I don't know why I follow him. Maybe because he's old enough to be my grandfather. Or maybe because I've spent over two months working beside him, day in and day out, at the group home and at the soup kitchen, and he's only ever made me laugh. Or maybe because, deep down, I trust him.

I know he'll give me good advice. An honest assessment. I know he'll give me the logic and the responses I wish my own parents would. But I can't talk to them about this. Again, Mom denied my request to have lunch or coffee together. At this rate, I can't talk to my parents about anything.

I wait as Buck locks up and then match his steps as we walk around the corner to an old-timey diner I've never been to.

Buck pulls the door open and shoots me a wink, letting me slip inside before him.

I grin when I see the way the diner is decked out. Black

and white checkered floor. Red vinyl barstools, bolted to the floor, in front of a throwback countertop. The servers are dressed in uniforms that resemble the style of the fifties. Or maybe the sixties?

"Hey, Amy," Buck greets the hostess.

Amy grins. "How's it going, Buck?"

"Same old," he chatters. "We'd like a booth if you've got one."

"Sure thing," she says, grabbing two menus and leading us to a corner.

I slide on one side. Buck takes the other.

I open my menu. He folds his hands on top of his.

After a minute of silence, I meet his gaze. "What?"

He shakes his head. "You gotta order the burger and milkshake," he reminds me.

I laugh, the first time today, and nod. Closing my menu, I place it down. "Okay, Buck. I'll have whatever you say."

"Good," he says cheerily. When the server stops at the end of our booth, Buck places our order. They're identical except my milkshake is vanilla and his is chocolate.

Then, he settles back in his seat and taps his clasped hands against the edge of the table. "What's his name, A?" he repeats.

I roll my eyes. "Derek."

Buck doesn't flinch. "Figured it was Reign."

"Because every girl in the country is obsessed with him?" I guess.

"Nah." Buck takes a napkin from the dispenser and wipes his hands. "Because when he's around, he can't tear his eyes away from you."

I draw in a sharp breath.

"Boy's sweet on you, Allegra."

"No, he's not," I say sadly.

Buck frowns. "What happened?"

At his concern, his sincerity, tears well in my eyes. I'm not used to this—someone truly caring about my feelings. Other than my friends at UCLA, no one in my life has showed this much compassion for me since...Levi. From before he became a Clover. From before he moved away and got famous and forgot he has a sister who adores him.

I clear my throat around the lump that formed there.

Buck passes me a napkin but doesn't comment on my tears.

I don't know why I tell him. Maybe it's because his eyes hold zero judgement. Maybe it's because I'm exhausted and have no one else to tell. But my mouth opens, and everything pours out.

The kiss on my seventeenth birthday. The stupid house rules and scaring away the boy at the pub. The kissing. The glances. The touches. The night in the alley—although, I don't give all the details, Buck certainly gets the point. And then, the social media image. Derek Reiner devastates me.

On top of that, the rest comes out. Levi inviting me on tour. My hesitation about going but also, my desire to connect with my brother. The agony of missing my family.

While I pour out my heart, our burgers and milkshakes arrive. We start to eat, in between my explanations and rambling monologues. Buck is silent the entire time, letting me get it all out. Letting me vent. Allowing me to release the pent-up pain I feel.

He gives me permission to fall apart. So, I do.

Over a burger and a milkshake, I recount my summer and take stock of my life. Of my path. Of where I started, where I'm at, and what I want next.

"He hurt you badly," Buck mutters when I'm done. "Both Levi and Reign."

I nod miserably.

"I don't know your brother well, but I've known Reign for a long, long time," Buck offers.

I arch an eyebrow, waiting.

"You ever think he's pushing you away for your own good?"

My mouth drops open.

Buck chuckles and lifts a hand in my direction. "Not really for your own good. But because he thinks it's for your own good?"

"I, he, what?" I ask, not following.

"You're an intelligent, compassionate, caring young woman, Allegra. Your heart is big, your soul deep, and your feelings vast."

I put down my burger.

"Derek is…complicated. He's loyal; I've seen that through his friendship with Dre. And he lives most of his life in the grey. Morally, socially, professionally. He sways whichever way he needs to go to ensure his survival. He has to; he's been on his own too long." Buck pauses to take a pull of his milkshake. To gather his thoughts and choose his words. "But that doesn't mean he doesn't have a code. He's got one and it's ironclad. Steadfast. His bandmate, one of his best friends, is your brother. And the band is his family. His survival. He keeps telling you you're too big for the life you're in, for your circumstances. You ever wonder if he means you're too big for him and his world too?"

Buck's words slam into me, raw and honest and threaded with a truth I never considered. With a possibility I want to reject. Because, to me, Derek is larger than life.

"Think about it," Buck counsels before I can argue. "You're moving forward. You're loving and compassionate and caring. You've got big dreams and a good head on your shoulders. Everyone who meets you knows you're going places. So does Reign. You just keep being yourself. If you compromise for him, he'll hate himself. And if I was a betting man, I'd say he's more scared of that than anything else. He hurt you, Allegra. But you could destroy him. You just don't realize it. You have no idea how much power a woman with your grace holds."

"Buck, I, I don't know what to say."

Buck smiles, his eyes crinkling in the corners. "You don't have to say anything, Allegra. Just think about it. And finish your milkshake."

I sputter out my second laugh of the day and do as Buck says.

"Thanks, Buck. I feel better," I admit. It's the truth. For the first time since I saw the image this morning, I feel balanced again.

Buck tips his head in my direction. "I'm always here for you, Allegra. No matter what, you've got me in your corner."

Again, the tears well in my eyes but I blink them back.

It feels like the homecoming I've spent the entire summer, maybe my entire life, searching for.

TWENTY
DEREK

After that night, Allegra ices me out. Her responses to my questions are clipped, one-word answers. She skims my touch, and meets my searching looks with blank expressions.

But her eyes are her giveaway. They've always been expressive, easy-to-read, even easier to desire. And behind their muted anger, hunger rages. I want it to consume me.

But things with the boys are finally right again. The band is hitting our summer stride, making good music, and gearing up to head overseas for our European tour. It's fast approaching—just a few more weeks and we'll be all over Europe.

Mav can't stop gushing about the girls.

Levi can't stop talking about the drugs.

Jameson can't stop whining about leaving Amelia behind.

And I...I don't know what I want anymore.

Maybe that's why I'm standing in the hallway, my arms crossed over my chest, waiting for Allegra to come out of the bathroom. I've taken up my post from the moment I heard the shower turn off. That was at least ten minutes ago.

What is she doing in there?

I glance down the hall. With my luck, Levi or Mav will lope by and wonder what the hell I'm doing, creeping on Allegra like this.

My jaw tics and I straighten my stance.

I hate the way she's looked at me over the past week. Looked through me. Like she can't bear to make eye contact. Like deep down, she resents me.

It's fucked, is what it is. I know I can't have her, but I can't let her go. Not entirely.

The bathroom door swings open and Allegra scurries through the doorway. A pale grey towel is wrapped around her body. Her hair is damp, hanging down her back and framing her face with waves and loose curls.

I step forward. "Allegra."

She freezes. Takes a moment to rearrange her expression. Glares at me. "What do you want?"

"To talk," I admit, my tone hoarse.

Her eyebrows dip and a flash of pain streaks across her face. It's shooting-star fast. If I had blinked, I'd have missed it.

My stomach twists painfully at the knowledge that I've hurt her. Deeper than I could have imagined.

"I miss you," I add, surprising myself with my honesty.

"I don't believe you," she whispers, her voice cracking.

I inch closer, and she retreats. My hand grazes her hip, my palm skimming the softness of her towel. "Yes, you do."

Her back meets the hallway wall, and she cranes her neck back to meet my eyes. "Why'd you do it?"

My heart thumps and my hand at her side closes into a grip, tugging on her towel and threatening to expose her.

Her arms remain limp at her sides, her eyes glued to mine. It's as if her nakedness would only be a distraction now. She doesn't care for any more distractions.

I sigh. "We were getting too close, Allegra. This"—I step into her, pressing the length of my body against hers—"is never going to be a thing."

"It already is," she counters, arching her chest into mine. She shudders and I know she wants the physical contact, the connection, as much as me.

I war with myself. "Not a real thing," I finally spit out. I want to warn her away just as badly as I want to rip the towel from her hot body and drop to my knees. Palm her ass and bring her sweet pussy to my mouth. Drink her nectar and feel her thighs quiver. Make her break on my tongue.

Heartbreak blossoms in her expression and she blinks slowly. I dip my head, breathe her in, vanilla and soap and sunshine. Fuck, I could get lost in my Stellina.

Her hands come up and slam into my chest, pushing me back. Since I wasn't expecting it, she catches me off guard, and I stumble. Scowl at her.

"Then stop playing games with me, Derek," she bites out, her voice low, her eyes flashing. "But I call bullshit. You want me. You want this." She gestures along her body.

My mouth drops open and her mouth twitches, more satisfaction than smile.

"I'm not the insecure seventeen-year-old girl you gave a first kiss to anymore," she hisses. Her towel loosens and she grips the fabric tighter to her side, keeping it in place. It dips slightly, showing more of her perky, rounded breasts. Her chest rises and falls, her panting in unison with her beats of anger. Hurt.

"I know what I want now. I know what I deserve." She shakes her head, flicks her fingers between us. "And you're right, this bullshit isn't it." With that, she turns on her heel and strides into her bedroom, closing the door behind her with a snick.

I listen as the lock catches and turns.

"Fuck." I scrub a hand over my face.

Then, I chuckle.

There's no way in hell Allegra doesn't want me.

But she's right, she deserves more than *this*. More than what I'm giving her.

More than what I'm capable of...

Can I ever give more? Can I ever be enough?

I stare at Allegra's closed bedroom door and wonder things I've never given myself permission to think before.

Allegra and me, as a real couple. Her body in my bed every night, her kiss on my lips every morning. Making her tea and watching movies. Her listening to my songs first, weighing in on the lyrics. Us together, always having each other's backs.

Heat sweeps through my limbs but it's more than base desire. It's longing. The sensation spreads, rolling and growing, yearning. The things I feel for her...can it be love? Can it be that pure and true? That real?

Could she feel that — that tenderness and longing and respect — for me?

I snap my mouth closed and press my lips together. Could I be the man she deserves? The man to give her what she wants? To truly love her?

"Yo!" Mav moves into the hallway. He gives me a strange look as he moves closer, then shakes his head.

I snap out of my trance. Out of the dumb thoughts that will never materialize.

No. I'm not the guy. Allegra isn't for me.

End of story.

"We're heading to the studio," Mav says, clipping my shoulder with his. "Then, the pub. Gotta go over some tour dates and plans for Europe!" He yells the last word and I know he's excited.

His enthusiasm is contagious, and I chuckle. "Sounds good, Mav. Let me change real quick."

"Do you, Reign," he agrees, knocking softly on his bedroom door.

When Allegra gives the all-clear, Mav slips inside. I hear their voices mingle, their laughter ring out.

No. There's no shot with Allegra Rousell.

Not when Europe beckons. Women in different countries. Women speaking different languages. Sold-out shows in capital cities. Afterparties. Free-flowing alcohol and passed-around pills.

I'd be a fool to drag her into that underworld. I've been a fool to keep this game going with her for so damn long.

Except, I don't know how to stop it. I can't lose. Or worse, surrender.

But I sure as hell can't win either.

THE TEN DAYS leading up to our European tour pass both slowly and quickly. Little bursts of energy, of constant movement and planning and packing, followed by lulls of restlessness.

I keep an eye on Allegra, watching without speaking. Posturing without proving anything. Searching but never seeking outright.

It's fucking torture. A slow burn, a desperate build. I clock her secret glances. Note her wary sidesteps. Despise the fall of her lips when I enter the room.

And yet, it's obvious I affect her. Probably live rent free in her mind. The same way she exists in mine, a constant I can't shut out.

With each passing day, we grow more brazen. Our stand-off softens. I skim my fingertips along the small of her back when she's at the kitchen sink, rinsing her coffee mug. She swipes her tongue across her bottom lip when I bound down the stairs, shirtless, my hair still damp from the shower. My knuckle catches the backside of her arm when she passes me in the hallway. Strands of her hair find purchase on my T-shirts in the laundry.

She's everywhere and nowhere. All-consuming and nothing.

Then, one night, she goes out with the BHH girls. I don't follow along like I mentally plan to. Instead, I spend the night buried in emails, disregarding another message from my so-called "father," and handling the fall-out of shifting show dates.

Mav's out, probably having a threesome. Levi's been fucked off his face since noon and is either passed out or still partying with Flip. The house is quiet. Peaceful and tranquil and the opposite of the type of homes I knew growing up.

I hook my heels on the bottom rung of the barstool, my notebooks and laptop spread over the butcher block island. It's nice, to work uninterrupted in a home I helped purchase. A headquarters for the band.

A legacy for the future.

I may have been born to a mother who loved heroin more than me and a father who didn't want me to begin with, but I figured it out. I may never deserve a woman like Allegra in my bed, in my life, but I'll be okay.

In the quiet of the kitchen, I accept that my present is

better than my past. That my future, with the whole continent of Europe beckoning, brighter still. The summer has been long and hot, with highs and lows, and a breathtaking surprise.

Allegra Rousell was a beautiful distraction. But now, September is fast approaching and she's going to move down a new path. I don't know what her plans are, but I doubt she'll stay in Boston. Maybe she'll head back to UCLA. Or move to New York.

She's intelligent, compassionate, and good. She'll figure it out.

I sigh, letting the tension in my neck melt into my shoulders. In another week, I'll be gone and the temptress that's invaded my waking moments as well as my dreams, a memory. Albeit a good one.

I chuckle to myself, and crack open the notebook with the lyrics I can't get just right.

You vanished like daybreak,
Lost stars and forgotten night.
You haunt me like a shadow,
Clingy and relentless.
You haunt me like her.

Her. I frown at the word and a strange sensation, heat and ice and unease, sweeps through my veins. I roll my lips together to hold back a groan. Brushing my thumb along the words, I realize the significance behind them.

Lost stars and forgotten night.
You haunt me like her.
Her.

Has this song been about Allegra, for Allegra, this entire time?

"Fuck." I crack my neck.

Have I been pining for her—keeping her high and safe on a damn pedestal—for most of my career?

Except...I'm clingy and relentless if this is how I internalized my exchanges with Allegra.

You haunt me like her.

Who? Her memory? Her ghost? She's leaving!

I grasp the sides of my head and tug on my hair.

The front door opens and I snap the notebook closed, my mind still reeling.

I turn and watch as Allegra stumbles inside. She's tipsy but adorable. A smile hugs her lips, and her hair is a wild mess of dark curls. She's rocking tiny black cut-off shorts and a simple T-shirt. She's got some jeans, a trench coat, and a long flowy dress folded over her arm. I frown, wondering what the clothes are for. Before I call out to ask, she deposits them on a chair by the front door and laughs. There's nothing pretentious about her. She doesn't try too hard, doesn't twist who she is to fit a mold.

She's unapologetically herself. Authentic. Sincere.

Perfect.

You haunt me like her.

Is this about the different versions of Allegra?

I tilt my head, envisioning the seventeen-year-old beauty who desired a first kiss. Blink. The sexy vixen who flipped my world upside down comes into focus. Blink. The woman I'm scared to admit I've fallen for — fucking crashed and burned beside — shimmers like an optical illusion.

"Derek," she gasps when she sees me, her hand pressing against her chest.

"Stellina," I reply, unable to stop myself. My voice catches and I clear my throat.

She's a bright star in a dark sky.

My North Star in a morally corrupt life.

You haunt me like her.

The realization soothes something deep inside my chest and I let out an exhale, feeling some of my frustration over this song, these lyrics, ease.

She shakes her head, as if to clear away the image of me. One eye closes as her other squints in my direction. Then, "What are you doing?"

I laugh and cross my arms over my chest. "Work. You?"

She discards her purse on a chair in the living room and walks closer. "Just had dinner and drinks with Claire and Vivi and some of the girls."

"How was it?"

She tilts her head. "Fun. Good. Makes me miss Kenny and Ivy and Nova but...I guess I'm just lucky to have many good friends."

"And friend groups," I point out, realizing that I only have my bandmates. And Dre. But I've been a lone wolf for a long time. As much as I like having a few trusted friends, I don't need them. Not the way Allegra requires social connections.

They don't fulfill me the way they do her; they only make me more tolerable to good people like her.

"Yeah," she agrees, a few steps away. "What are you working on?"

I turn on the barstool, until I'm facing her. My knees part, making room for her between my legs, and she steps between them.

"Song lyrics."

She rolls her eyes, not surprised. "Sing them for me."

I lean back slightly, catch the look in her gaze. She's sober enough to know what she's asking and yet, I want to give it to her. Give in to her. My hands settle on her hips and I give a squeeze before I sing for her. Just the one verse that haunts me as much as she has. As much as she will when she's gone.

You vanished like daybreak,
Lost stars and forgotten night.
You haunt me like a shadow,
Clingy and relentless.
You haunt me like her.

Allegra presses her lips together and rests her hands on my shoulders. They slip along the material of my tank before clasping at the back of my neck. "Is it about me?" she whispers. "Lost stars and forgotten night? Clingy and relentless?"

"I'm the relentless one," I admit. "And yeah, Stellina, it's about you. I'm still working through it."

"It's beautiful. Even the haunting part," she murmurs. "Sad, too." Her expression is thoughtful, her voice low.

The heat from her body presses into my palms and I grip her tighter. An irrational thought plagues me. She's leaving; she's going to slip away. I've known it all along and yet it knocks into me like a crashing wave.

I don't want to say good-bye. How will I ever let her go?

"Do you forgive me?" I ask, my voice raw.

Allegra stares at me, her expression naked, her eyes brimming with emotion. "I don't like feeling angry," she admits. "It's...exhausting."

"Sometimes," I agree. "But it protects you more than vulnerability."

"Maybe. In the short term," she cedes.

I dip my head, seeing her point. She's right and I like that even a little tipsy she can best me. "So, we're good?" *Please let us be okay.*

Her eyes hold mine, piercing in their intensity. She

shrugs. "I care about you too much for us not to be good. Even though sometimes I wish we were nothing at all."

Her honesty peels back my bravado. She plucks my heartstrings and gives me a flash of those thoughts I know better than to think. When I cup her cheek, she leans into my palm. When I grip her waist, she inches closer, until her inhales drag her breasts across my abdomen.

"Don't burn out, Stellina," I whisper, right before my mouth touches hers.

She lifts her face in response, kissing me back with a candidness I revel in. One I admire but never allow myself to show.

Allegra will always best me. Because she's right.

In the long term, vulnerability trumps anger.

TWENTY-ONE
ALLEGRA

His kiss is dizzying. His mouth a current I'm helpless against. Derek pulls me in as easily and quickly as he did the first time. And the second. And the time after that.

His thighs part and I press myself as close as I can get. His body heat seeps into my skin as his hand tightens on my waist, slips to my hip, rolls around to palm my ass.

I moan lightly. My fingers curl into the top of his shoulder while my other hand slides up his back, over his neck, my fingers slipping through the short hair on the back of his head.

I pull him even closer, wanting to lose myself in this moment. In this kiss.

Because it's different than the frantic need against the brick wall in the alley.

It's nothing like the night he took my mouth, desperate and needy, beside the stove.

This kiss holds hints of our first kiss. Sweet and sincere. Magic.

Derek's tongue sweeps inside my mouth, touching mine. Dancing.

I grip him harder, and he folds over me, clutching me to his chest as his kiss drugs and drowns me in the sweetest of oblivions.

The last of our cold front melts. Our posturing proves pointless. The battle of wills we've silently raged for weeks clashes together, culminating in this moment.

I don't want to push him away. I don't want to burn from his rejection.

I want Derek. This kiss. This night.

He slides from the barstool, towering over me. But he keeps his mouth fused to mine, his hands kneading up and down my body, as if he wants to touch every inch of my skin.

My breasts grow heavy as my breathing kicks up. Derek's touch is gentle as he cups my right breast, squeezes. Then, he pulls back and looks at me. His eyes search mine, asking permission.

Silently, I lift my arms and he lets out a shaky exhale. But his fingers hook underneath the hem of my shirt, and he slowly drags the thin material up my frame, clearing my head, and dropping it on top of his laptop behind me.

He leans back, his eyes taking their fill. "You're gorgeous, Allegra," his says seriously. His fingertips run along the swells of my breasts, and he watches, mesmerized, as goose bumps dot my skin in the wake of his touch.

Then, he reaches for the clasp in between my breasts and in one expert move, pops it open. My breasts spill free, but his hands are there to catch them. A perfect handful for his grasp. His thumbs flick over my nipples, massaging them, as my bra hangs off my arms.

"Perfect," Derek murmurs, dropping a kiss to the side of my neck. "You're so fucking perfect, baby. So goddamn pure."

Heat pools between my thighs as a delicious ache spreads through my pelvis. My hips lift, seeking out his length. Knowing what I want, Derek shuffles closer. His mouth drags along the column of my neck, kissing a path up from my collarbone to the sensitive spot behind my ear. The entire time, his hands are on my breasts, kneading and touching. My hips tilt up again and this time, he presses his hard, impressive length, against the inside of my thigh.

I nearly shudder, wishing he would press against my core. Give me some friction. Give me some relief.

Instead, he turns his torso, dragging his hardness against my thigh again.

"You wet for me, Allegra?" he taunts.

I nod.

"Give me the words, beautiful. Want to hear you say them." His teeth nip at my earlobe.

"Yes," I breathe out.

"How wet, love?"

"So, oh God, wet. I, I'm, Derek," I manage, half delirious. Between the buzz in my bloodstream and the desire pooling in my nether regions, I'm half incoherent.

"Yeah," he murmurs, his hand sliding down my stomach.

I watch as his fingers trail to the waistband of my shorts. He pops the button and shimmies them down my ass. Once they clear my hips, they drop to the floor, and I kick them to the side.

It dawns on me that I'm wearing nothing but a black lace thong and Derek is fully clothed. I have no idea how far we're taking this, but I know it needs to be more equitable.

I grasp the material of his tank top and he chuckles, whipping it off in an instant.

Derek takes my palm and presses it to the center of his

chest. "Have your way with me, Allegra," he taunts. "Whatever you want to do, beautiful."

Then his lips are on mine. His fingers hook underneath the waistband of my thong and he drags the backs of his fingernails along the seam, back and forth over my lower abdomen.

My hands explore his abdomen and pecs. His coiled muscles and hot skin. I slide my palms over his shoulders and down his arms. I wrap my arms around his frame and grab his ass. I touch him the way I've dreamed of, imagined, fantasized about, for years.

Time stretches and stands still. Derek and I are wrapped in our cocoon, in our truce, oblivious to everything but each other.

I touch my tongue to his, tasting and taking. He dips his fingers into my panties, a whisper away from the place I want his touch. I lift up on my tippy toes, encouraging him.

He chuckles. "Don't rush me, Stellina. I want to savor this with you."

I melt at his words, wondering if he means them.

Enough to want to repeat them tomorrow.

Before I can decide if we should take this further, if this is a good idea at all or if we've already fucked everything up, a sharp voice bellows in the quiet.

"What the fuck are you doing?" Mav rushes Derek, shoving him away from me.

He stumbles to the side as I shriek and jump back. Except the kitchen island is at my back so there's nowhere to go.

"Mav!" I cry out, throwing an arm toward him.

He throws my clothes in my face instead. "Get dressed, Allegra." Mav points at Derek, not looking at me. "Don't you fucking touch her. Don't even look at her."

Derek tosses his hands up in a surrender position, backing away from Mav. He shoots me an apologetic look.

What is he sorry for?

That Mav interrupted us?

That we got caught?

That we started this in the first place?

Now that his hot body isn't pressed against mine, confusion infiltrates my mind.

"What the hell are you thinking?" Mav backs Derek up into the living room.

I quickly pull on my shorts and T-shirt, forgoing my thong and bra. I follow the boys.

"Mav," I say.

He ignores me.

"She's Levi's sister," Mav bellows.

Derek winces and I recoil into myself.

"She's my roommate," Mav continues. "She's not one of your good-time girls. She's a good fucking girl." He shoves Derek's shoulder. "But you couldn't keep it in your pants, could you? You always screw everything up because you don't know when to quit. You're insatiable. Every fucking part of you wants more. Isn't this enough?" He throws an arm wide to encompass the living room, the brownstone, Boston. "You had to fuck with her?" Mav's finger jabs in my direction.

"Mav," I say quietly, "it's not like that." Do I tell him about our past? About my seventeenth birthday? About how Levi invited me on tour, to Europe? I frown. Didn't Levi tell them that I'm coming? My eyes snap to the clothes I deposited on the chair by the front door. Claire lent me some items for September in Europe, knowing I'm low on funds and didn't pack much for my summer in Boston. I'm hoping to hit Levi up for a winter jacket but...

A new horror skates up my arms. Does my brother remember he invited me on tour or is he so messed up, he forgot?

"No," Derek clips. "Mav's right. I, fuck." He scrubs a hand over his face. "I crossed a line. I never should have disrespected you like that, Allegra. Not in the kitchen." His eyes find mine, bleeding with remorse.

Regret because he touched me?

Or because it's out in the open now?

"I'm sorry," Derek mutters.

And it's the worst thing he could have said. His apology cuts, burning a path of shame through my center.

He's sorry…?

"For which part?" I bite out, having déjà vu. How many times are we going to take two steps forward just to leap back again?

Mav's face spins toward me, confusion evident in his expression.

I ignore him and keep my eyes trained on Derek.

"For all of it," he rasps out. His eyes close in defeat.

My stomach sinks and my chest tightens. I wish I still felt drunk, from alcohol or lust. From anything.

"Whatever," I bite out. I'm not doing this in front of Mav. "I'm tired. I'm going to bed."

Clasping my thong and bra in my hand, I scoop up Claire's clothes, and take the stairs up to the bedroom I share with Mav.

I hover outside my brother's bedroom door. Did he mean it when he invited me on tour? Does he want to work on our relationship and erase the space between us like he said?

Will Derek want me on tour? Three hours ago, I didn't

care. An hour ago, I would have said hell yes. Now, I'm not sure.

I just know that in another week, everything will be different. Everything is changing.

Even that doesn't provide relief because it means this—all of this—will be over.

Summer is ending and with it, this familiarity I've formed with the guys. Living in their Boston brownstone is completely different than being on tour, in Europe, where they're performing and practicing and preparing.

Except, maybe Europe will be better?

Maybe being on the road will give Derek and me time to explore what's between us. We'll be in close quarters, without our usual routine to rely on. My brother invited me for a reason. Does he miss me as much as I miss him?

My head spins and exhaustion, bone-deep and soul crushing, settles over me.

I change for bed and slip under the covers.

But sleep doesn't find me. How can it when Mav and Derek argue late into the night?

Their clipped voices make me feel worse.

Even though I know, deep down, Derek and I are what we are, this is one of those times I wish we were nothing at all.

TWENTY-TWO
DEREK

"You can't tell him." I glare at Mav.

"Really? Why not?" Mav shoots back. "Doesn't he have a right to know that you're fucking—"

"I never fucked her," I bite out.

Mav winces and I swear.

I hate that we're speaking about Allegra this way. It's vulgar and complicated and awful.

"Why'd you do it, Reign?" Mav asks.

Our conversation has gone in circles for the past thirty minutes. We've argued and verbally sparred. We've hurled insults and razor-sharp words.

But it all comes back to this.

"Why?" he asks again, shaking his head. His eyes are clouded with disappointment, and I feel it because I know how much Mav cares for Allegra. He loves her like a sister and feels protective of her.

It grants me relief as much as it pisses me off. I like that she has him watching out for her. That Mav will step in to protect Allegra, even when I can't. Especially when she needs protecting from me.

But fuck, if I wanted to deck him for cockblocking me tonight. Especially because tonight wasn't about the physical. My emotions were on high alert, lingering and flaring up at the chance.

She looked so cute when she stumbled into the house earlier. I wanted to press myself against her and let some of her good, some of that innocence, seep into my skin.

And that kiss. The fact that Allegra Rousell could want a man like me, it's empowering. Heady. Blows my damn mind.

I want to wrap myself in Allegra's sweetness, hold it to my chest like a cloak, and lose myself in her. I want us both to surrender to the moment, to each other.

That was finally happening. Tonight, the bitter front we've kept up for the past two weeks was changing into some type of resignation. Acceptance. The next natural expression in a chain of events that keeps guiding us back to each other.

Our searching mouths and desperate hands.

Fucking Maverick Tate.

I glare at my friend. "You don't know what you're talking about. It's different with her."

Mav stumbles back half a step, as if my words physically affect him. Surprise blooms in his expression, quickly followed by doubt. His eyes narrow and his mouth twists. "You're bullshitting me."

I sigh, running my palm over my head. I grip the back of my neck until it aches. "Allegra and me...there's always been something there," I add, not willing to tell him how much. And for how long.

It's none of his damn business and while I usually don't give a shit if my bandmates, or the world, know who I'm fucking, Allegra's different. She has been from day one.

Stellina. Mine.

Mav swears and shakes his head. "Reign, we're about to head out on tour."

I look at him, pausing at the severity of his expression. He looks...disturbed. Worried in a way that worries me.

"The band," Mav starts, stops, swears. "We're hanging on by a thread."

I drop into a nearby chair and Mav collapses into the couch. "What do you mean? We're finally jiving again. The past week—"

"The music's been sick," he cuts me off, agreeing. "The new songs you wrote have been incredible."

"So, what's the problem?" I pitch forward, dropping my elbows to my knees.

Mav shakes his head. "You really live in your own world."

"Say what you've gotta say, Mav," I snap, losing my patience. I'm not here for a therapy session.

"Levi's on the brink of needing rehab. You know that, right?" Mav dips his head, trying to catch my eyes.

I stare at him and at the concern in his pale blue gaze, I think back to the past few months. Levi's hot and cold attitude. The way he didn't embrace his sister the way I thought he would've this summer. His dumb mind games with Cynthia.

How often he's high...all the damn time. The pills and calls to Flip and partying...

"You party all the time," I point out but there's no accusation in my tone.

"Yeah, but I'm fucked up in different ways," Mav admits. There's no pain in his voice either, just a blatant assessment of what is.

If I was a feeling guy, if I was Allegra, his statement

would break my heart. Instead, it causes a thread of discomfort to pull tight through my limbs and I shift my weight again.

"Levi's about to spiral," Mav warns, sounding wise considering he's the youngest in the group. He's practically Allegra's age, for fuck's sake. "My brother is going to struggle, being away from Amelia."

"That fucking cunt," I mutter.

"She's gonna mess with his head, the way she always does," Mav continues. Now that he's started, he's rattling off issues with ease. How long has he been worried about this tour? How long has he kept these concerns to himself?

While I've been focused on the music, the one song I can't get right, the lyrics and the flow and the performance dates, Mav's been shouldering the burden of the band. Of the messes we constantly make and the scrapes we find ourselves in.

"All we need is one match, one spark, and the whole thing is gonna go up in flames." Mav's gaze is steely. Certain. "You fuck with, hurt, even confuse Allegra, and there's gonna be issues. Big ones." He holds his hands out to the sides to indicate how colossal of a screw-up this is. Does he mean Levi or himself? Or the whole band?

In one summer, Allegra Rousell became the Clovers' sweetheart. Hell, Boston's sweetheart. Dre's best girl. Buck's best friend. She's got an in with the BHH girls.

Fuck. "You're right." The words are dragged from my mouth, like gum that's stuck to the back of my throat, stretching and contorting, and a little painful.

"Don't mess with the delicate balance we've got going," Mav advises. "Let her go. Summer's ending. She's leaving anyway."

My eyes snap back to his. "Where's she going?"

Mav shrugs. "I don't know. I assume back to LA. To her life. And we're going on tour. The only way things work between you and A is if you wifey her up."

My mouth drops open as horror explodes in my chest. Wifey her up? I'll ruin her.

Mav shakes his head. "I don't mean put a ring on her finger. I mean, make her yours. For keeps. No more fucking around. Go on tour and keep it in your pants. Spend your nights with your phone pressed to your ear, telling her about your day, instead of out with the crew. Become Jameson." Mav winces at the mention of his brother.

For the first time in my life, I feel a flicker of sympathy for my bandmate. He was one of my first friends, but Jameson and I never clicked the way Levi and I do. We didn't have that instant rapport of creating music off each other, like we could both see the end and knew where the other was trying to go.

Jameson is talented. He lends a steadiness to the group, a foundation, that the rest of us would likely knock over before we figured out how to build up. Jameson helps us build.

"That's not going to happen," Mav says gently.

I know he's right. I'm not cut out to be a Jameson. I'm not going to spend my days glued to my phone or text messages and neatly drop into my bed after sold-out shows.

I care about Allegra but I'm not ready to wifey her up.

"No, you're right," I admit quietly, coming to terms with the fact that I have to truly let her go.

Why did she come this summer?

In the four years since I kissed her, she's crossed my mind a handful of times. I sought her out on social media two or three times each year. Every now and then, I'd ask

Levi how his sister is doing, what Allegra's up to. But I didn't let it stop me from living. I kept her alive in a back corner of my mind and I moved on.

Except this time, I know that will be impossible.

There's something about Allegra that calls to me. She makes me believe that I can have more, be better, be...worth it. Her. And it's the most powerful and dangerous belief to cross through my mind.

"Let her go with some dignity, Reign," Maverick mutters. "She's a good girl and she's finally found a path she loves. She had a good summer. Let her end it on a high note."

"Yeah," I mumble. "Of course. You're right, mate."

Mav sighs. He takes no joy in being right, not about this.

In this moment, I realize what a good friend Maverick Tate is. For years, he's been the kid brother of our group. The goof. But at his core, he's a solid guy. He just doesn't let anyone see it. Keeps those parts hidden behind his humor and charm.

The front door bangs open, and Mav and I jump.

Levi sways in the doorframe. He shuffles forward a few steps and kicks the front door closed.

Gripping the back of the chair, he straightens and surveys the room. When he spots us, a grin cuts his face. His dark eyes, similar to Allegra's, flash. "Hey, fuckers! What're you getting into?"

Mav sighs again. Standing, he helps ease Levi into a chair and moves to the kitchen to fill a glass of water for him.

Levi drops his head back and stares at the ceiling.

I study my best friend. He's plastered, fucked off his face. But he's also functioning the way I'd expect because...

how long has it been since Levi *hasn't* been fucked off his face?

We've grown apart this summer, but I didn't fully acknowledge it until this moment. I've been so wrapped up in my own life, in the song I can't perfect, in battling the feelings I have for Allegra, that I didn't notice Levi is slipping.

Mav passes him the glass and Levi takes a long pull of water, smacking his lips together. "Ready for tour?" he asks us, his gaze—wild and unfocused and glazed—bouncing between Mav and me. "It's gonna be sick. All that pussy. All those clubs. Fucking sold-out shows." He shakes his head as if it's unfolding in his mind. "Rome and London. Fucking Paris. Just like when we were kids." He laughs.

Mav shoots me a look. *What the hell is he talking about? When we were kids?*

I shrug.

"It's gonna be awesome, man," Mav says.

"Yeah." Levi nods, tapping his fingertips against the armrest. "Yeah." He cuts a grin, his face flushed. "My sister's always wanted to see Paris."

I start at the mention of Allegra. And Paris? I didn't know that. I guess she didn't study abroad or anything. Shame, she'd love Paris. Hell, she'd love anywhere new and brimming with possibility.

Look how she flourished in one summer in Boston.

"It's gonna be the best now that she's coming," Levi announces, his grin growing.

To be honest, he looks kind of creepy. But it's his words, more than his face, that give me pause.

"Coming where?" Dread fills my veins. Fuck off, Levi.

"To...on tour?" Mav asks.

Levi nods. Squints. "Didn't I tell you guys?"

"Nope," Mav replies.

Levi shakes his head. "Damn. She said yes. I mean, of course she did."

My legs feel heavy and my stomach sinks at Levi's casual dropping of this bomb in my fucking lap. Mav glares at me and it detonates.

The disaster explodes in my face.

"I wanna fix shit with her, ya know?" Levi rambles. "I've been a shit brother this summer and A deserves more. Hell, she deserves the whole damn world. I wanna take her to Paris..." He keeps talking but I tune him out.

Because her face flickers in my mind.

Deep, soulful brown eyes. Her playful smirk. Taunting words.

Four years ago, I kissed Allegra Rousell and something inside of me clicked with her. Something changed or rearranged, and I felt the first flicker of hope.

Tonight, I had my hands in her hair and my mouth on her neck and I wanted it all...everything, with her.

Mav glares at me and I know what he's silently communicating.

You gotta end it. This has to stop. One match, the whole fucking band disintegrates...

Levi chatters animatedly, his hands gesticulating.

Fuck, I've gotta break his sister's heart.

I have to let Allegra go.

Not with my stupid games. Not by pissing her off and reeling her back in. Not with one step forward, two steps back.

I need to cut ties and let her go so I don't ruin the band. So I don't destroy her on tour.

So I don't collapse under the knowledge that I'll never be enough.

Levi's right; Allegra Rousell deserves the world.

I'm too broken and fucked up to offer a slice of that.

I can't even give her Paris.

TWENTY-THREE
ALLEGRA

The next two days pass in a blur. Mainly because I'm so lost in my thoughts, my mental grip on reality loosens.

Is going on tour a mistake? Does Levi really want me to join? Is my presence creating friction among the group?

Mav will barely meet my eyes. Derek avoids me at all costs.

And Levi...my brother wanders through his day with one foot already in the evening, anticipating the fun and trouble waiting for him.

Will my presence on tour give Levi the support he needs? Or will I enable him to continue down the dark and dangerous path he's traveling?

Will I offer a constant stability to Derek's chaotic life? Or will I break my heart trying to keep up with his?

I don't have any answers. Less now than I did when I withdrew from UCLA. In terms of my personal life, I am truly lost.

However, my time spent at the group home and food shelter are the brightest spots in the bleakest of days. I may not know what my future holds but I know I want to pursue work that fills my cup. I want to be part of a team—like Dre's, like Vivi's—and give back to a community that matters. Like Buck's.

At least this summer in Boston gave me clarity in one aspect of my life.

The thought makes me smile as I pack the jeans and dress Claire lent me into my suitcase. I snap a photo of the trench coat and send it to the group chat.

Nova: Ooh, I love that trench! Is that Burberry?

Me: Claire lent it to me.

Ivy: You may have made better friends in Boston than us...

Kenny: Hush! We're great friends.

Nova: I'd never gift any of you my Burberry anything...

Me: It's not designer but great quality! I'm packing.

Kenny: You're really going?

Nova: Stop confusing her, Mckenna! She already committed. Right, A?

Ivy: Yes! She's not a commitment-phobe like you, Nova.

Me: (laughing face emoji) I'm going. I'm committed. I'm packing.

Nova: What else did Claire lend you?

I snap a photo of the jeans and dress in my suitcase.

Ivy: Ooh, great pattern on the dress.

Nova: We should bring Claire into our group. We could use her style input...

Kenny: What else do you need?

Me: A winter coat...

Nova: I've got 2 at my dad's in France! I'll get him to post them to you when you land in London. Or you can swing by his place and dig through my closet there?

Me: That would be amazinggggg! Thank you, Nova!

Ivy: See? We're good friends!

Nova: Sometimes. (smirking emoji face)
Me: I miss you, girls! Promise we'll meet in Europe?
Nova: Duh.
Ivy: Promise.
Kenny: I'll try my best.
Me: (three red heart emojis)

Tossing down my phone, I tuck my hair behind my ears and continue to pack. Knowing that my friends will meet me in Europe soothes my nerves and eases some of my fears. I may not recognize Levi or know what to do with Derek, but I have great friends in my corner. I have something tangible to offer to my workplace. To the kids that have buried themselves in my heart. I know what I want for my future. That is already enough.

With that comforting thought in mind, I head downstairs for breakfast. I haul my suitcase with me as I want to drop it by the front door beside the guys' packed bags. The house is quiet. I imagine my brother is still passed out, sleeping off whatever drink he dove into last night. Mav's bed was empty and Derek's usually out early—either at the gym or the studio.

I walk down the stairs slowly, dragging my fingertips along the scuffed wall. This house has been a sanctuary this summer and I'm going to miss its worn-in and well-loved space. Its warm embrace. The way it houses and cares for the most rambunctious and ambitious group of men I know.

When I reach the kitchen, I make an espresso and pop a bagel in the toaster. As I sit at the kitchen island, I close my eyes and inhale. Gather as many memories and moments from this kitchen, this summer, and imprint them on my mind.

Will the tour in Europe heal my fractured relationship

with Levi or make it worse? Will it clarify my confusion about Derek or twist my thoughts even more?

What will I do afterward? Search for a job or re-enroll in UCLA?

It feels like I'm teetering on the edge of a precipice. One gentle breeze, just a stirring, and I'll fall. One way, or the other.

For some reason, each step forward holds a heaviness that I already feel around my neck. On top of my shoulders. The pressure and the weight of it is waiting. But which step do I take? Which direction do I choose? Is one truly better than the other?

My bagel pops up and I jump at the sound. Laughing at myself, I pull out the hot bagel, drop it on a plate, and move to the refrigerator for some strawberry jam.

A knock sounds on the front door and I pause, listening intently.

It sounds again and I reroute my steps to the front door. It's unusual for someone to knock this early. And, given the security out front, not many have access to the brownstone.

I glance out the window and grin when I see Dre on the porch. Pulling the door wide open, I beckon him inside. "Hey! Good morning. Come on in; I'm just making breakfast. Are you hungry?"

Dre lifts his head and the heartbreak in his eyes glues me in place.

The grey morning light casts him in somber hues, and his face tells a story of tragedy. My limbs lock down and panic crawls up my throat. It scrambles quickly but when I open my mouth, a wail doesn't emerge. Instead, a whisper. "What's wrong?"

My heart beats in my temples, slowly, loudly. Deafeningly.

Dre shuffles on the porch. His eyes are red-rimmed and bloodshot. Exhaustion clings to the edges of his lips, pinching the corners of his mouth. He looks like he wants to fall apart but can't until he shares the news. Splits the burden.

I shake my head, not wanting to hear whatever he's going to say next. Because whatever words comes out of his mouth are going to gut me. I already know it; I want no part of it.

Self-preservation kicks in but I don't fight. Or fall. Instead, I beg, "Dre."

"I'll come in," he agrees, stepping inside the house. He closes the door behind him, and I move toward the kitchen, needing the normalcy of my routine. I'll make him a coffee. It's something to do with my hands. A task to focus my attention on.

Dre moves silently but I feel him behind me. I know he's in the kitchen, shadowing my moves. Waiting for me to catch up so he can share whatever he came here to say.

I spin toward him and toss my hands in the air. Helpless. My body trembles with the knowledge that *knowing* is painful. But now that Dre's here, the morning has twisted sideways, and I can't not *know* either.

Dre pulls me into his arms. A giant bear of a hug from an imposing, generous man.

"Buck had a heart attack," he murmurs into my ear.

I start to pull back, violently, as if the strength of my reaction can counteract the truth of his words. Dre grips me harder. Holds me closer. Hugs me tighter.

"He died instantly. No pain. No suffering," Dre continues, his tone soothing, his words low. Their meaning, a strange type of gift I cling to, even though I'd prefer to reject their validity.

No pain. No suffering.
A heart attack.

My body folds in on itself. All strength leaves my limbs in a giant whoosh, on an exhale. I stagger but Dre catches me, takes all my body weight, and gathers me to his chest. He sinks to his knees, taking me with him, until I'm a lifeless rag doll, half in his lap, half on the kitchen floor.

His arms are strong, his chest solid. He cups the back of my head and makes a soft shushing sound. It takes me a second to realize that the keening, the howl, is coming from me.

From deep within my soul.

My heart cracks and my spirit breaks. The kitchen swirls around me, dark colors and shadows. My fingers tremble and my eyes burn.

"He loved you, A," Dre says.

My cheeks are slippery with tears. I press my face into Dre's chest, my head tucked under his chin, and fall apart. My shoulders shake with sobs as the loss, the grief, of Buck hits me like a tidal wave. It sucks my strength from my limbs, like a leech, and leaves me drowning. Unraveling. Gasping for air and reaching for a surface I can't see.

"You brought him joy in such a short amount of time."

I squeeze my eyes shut and wail.

"Like the daughter he always wanted."

My fingers curl in the bottom of Dre's T-shirt.

"Thank you, for giving that to him."

My shoulders shake and nausea twists my intestines.

The pain is excruciating. The loss is unbearable.

"He told me you went for burgers and milkshakes." Dre makes a tiny sound, half snort, half sob. It vibrates against my forehead. "That was special for him."

"I didn't, I wasn't, was he sick?" I sputter. My mouth is dry, my tongue too thick to properly form words.

"No," Dre mutters. "No. This was sudden. No one saw it coming."

I pull back slightly, wiping my hands across my cheeks. They come away wet and smeared with makeup. Shimmer and sparkle that look more out of place than I feel.

Right now, my grief overpowers everything.

"I'm sorry, Dre," I say, staring right at him. "I'm so sorry."

His eyes are shadowed with pain, his expression grim. Still, he held me up. He even came here to tell me the news.

Dre shakes his head and I take his hand. Squeeze. I want to give him a sliver of comfort. I want him to know that he's not alone. I feel his pain; I loved Buck too.

"He was like a father to me too," he offers, his voice breaking.

I nod, knowing what he means. Even though my dad is alive and well, he's barely spoken to me since I left for UCLA. It's been over three years since we sat together, talking and sharing and laughing.

This summer, Buck gave me a gift. And now, it's gone, just like him.

"I found him this morning. Early," Dre continues. One side of his mouth lifts. "He was already at the soup kitchen. Preparing for the day, for the people. Buck was the best man I knew."

I nod, wondering what his final moments were like. I hope Dre was right. No pain. No suffering. I pray his death was peaceful and easy. Like slipping into a long-yearned-for dream. Like closing your eyes. One final blink and—oh!

But the thought of going to the soup kitchen, to the group home and telling the kids who adore Buck, to walking past the diner—it all seems impossible. I shake my head; I can't think about anything beyond this moment.

"What can I help with?" I offer.

Dre shakes his head. "You're too good, little girl. Too bright and too compassionate for this."

You're too big for this world.

The words echo, oddly familiar. No more comforting than the first time I heard them.

I don't understand the *"this"* Dre refers to but I don't press him for an explanation. Does he mean this work? This loss? This day?

"There's not much to help with," he clarifies. "Buck left a will and his wishes are simple. He's an organ donor and wants to be cremated. Spread with the wind, over the water, and laid to rest in our hearts, in our work, in the legacy he helped create, more than anything else."

I nod along, seeing Buck's personality, his love and laughter and heart, in the simple sending-away Dre describes.

"When?" I croak.

Dre shakes his head. Offers a watery smile. "Don't worry, A. He wouldn't want you to miss Paris."

I shake my head. "I wasn't even thinking—"

"I know." Dre reaches for me. Pulls me into another hug. "But I'm telling you," he continues, his mouth by my ear. "Buck would want you to live. To soar. To go and experience and love. Don't let opportunities pass you by. Don't sleepwalk through your life. Embrace it with every part of yourself. Give everything you've got to the present." He kisses my temple. "Go to Europe, Allegra. And live it."

"What the hell is going on?" Derek's voice interrupts our moment. His tone is hard, his words accusatory.

Dre turns slowly. We both look up at Derek and when

he sees our expressions, notes my tears, his anger bleeds away. A stoic kind of blankness washes over his face and he turns his back, grips the edge of the kitchen island. Whirls around. "Who?" he spits.

"Buck," Dre says softly.

"Fucking hell," Derek swears, striding to the window. He slams his palms down on either side of the sink and gazes out into the morning grey. It's overcast and sullen today. Threatening rain. Maybe even thunder and lightning.

It's as if the sky, the universe, God himself, is on the precipice of mourning Buck along with us.

An entire cosmic shift to pay homage to a man with a too-big smile and a too-soft heart.

Dre and Derek talk in hushed voices. At some point, Dre disentangles himself and stands.

But I remain huddled on the floor. A ball of loss, a mess of grief, a puddle of tears. They continue to come, relentless. Sad and angry and disbelieving.

My knees cut into the cold tiles. My hands grow numb.

And still I sit, waiting for the grey day to roll over me and drag me under. Drown me for good.

TWENTY-FOUR
DEREK

She's dead weight in my arms but feels like a sack of feathers. Allegra's head rolls against my shoulder and her feet catch on the doorframe before I maneuver her up the stairs.

Her eyes are flat. Her expression blank. Empty.

She's hurting and the pain is so intense, that her body is protecting her the best way it can. Even while her mind sifts through various degrees of anguish.

"He's gone," she murmurs, her eyes finding mine. "He really saw me, you know."

"I know," I mutter because Buck saw everyone.

Right down to your core, he knew your worth. The good, the bad, the ugly. But he never judged you for it. There was a quiet acceptance in his gaze, a knowing understanding in his tone.

He gave whatever he could and loved you through the rest.

I knew Allegra and Buck connected this summer. It's impossible to know Buck, or Allegra, and not migrate toward their light. But I didn't realize how tight they were.

It wasn't until Dre filled me in that I realized Buck stepped into the shoes of a father figure for Allegra. Much like he did for Dre.

I didn't realize they had burgers and milkshakes. I didn't know Allegra shared her concerns and fears, her plans and mistakes. I didn't know any of it. She told him about Europe. Did she confide in him about me? Did he know I lured her in all summer, just to cast her away?

Did he despise me for it? Or understand, like always?

I hate that I wasn't there for her this summer as she tried to navigate her new normal. I hate that tomorrow morning, we're boarding a flight to London. We're closing this season out, ending this chapter, and starting something new.

And I fucking despise that I'm going to have to tell her good-bye, to tell her we're really over, even though she's joining us.

Mav is right; the band won't survive the upheaval of Allegra and me together. Not unless I make it right and I'm not capable of doing that. I know it, so why bother trying?

I feel sick at the thought of causing her more pain, more tears. But that's for later.

I shake my head. Shut down my shitty thoughts.

Right now, she *needs* me.

In this moment, I can be present. I'm capable of manning up to give her the comfort and assurance she craves. For the next handful of hours, I can be the man she deserves.

I shuffle from one foot to the next outside her bedroom door. Is Mav inside sleeping? Will he be home soon? Will he pump Allegra for info or force her to talk about things she's not ready to discuss?

I glance down at her. She holds my gaze and shakes her head slightly. I nod my understanding and carry her to my bedroom. I kick the door closed behind me and place Allegra down in the center of my bed. She lies flat on her back, staring up at the ceiling.

What do her eyes see? What is she thinking?

"Hey," I say softly. I peel her socks off her feet and drop them to the floor.

She turns onto her side, her knees lifting into her chest, her cheek pressed into my pillow.

"I'm so fucking sorry, Stellina." I pull my comforter over her small frame, tuck her in.

She doesn't respond but tears gather in the corners of her eyes. Her mascara is smeared, her lips puffy, and still, she's gorgeous. My heart twists and I wonder what the fuck it says about me that I find her beautiful when she cries.

I reach out and drag the pads of my fingertips over her cheek, underneath her eye, around the shell of her ear.

"You want to sleep?" I ask.

She shakes her head. "Not tired."

I nod, understanding the helplessness that grips her.

I've felt it before. In foster care. When Simon would beat me, my mind would drift away, to another world entirely, even though part of me remained tethered to the moment.

After, when the band blew up and I found myself surrounded by people but acutely alone, that helplessness resurfaced.

You're exhausted but your mind races.

You're reckless but there's nowhere to channel the energy.

I toe off my sneakers and round to the other side of the bed. Slipping underneath the covers, I wrap my arm around Allegra's waist and hold her close, pulling until her back collides with my chest.

My hips cradle Allegra's. My knees kiss the back of hers, our thighs pressed together. My hand splays wide in the middle of her stomach. She arches her back slightly, snuggling closer, but it drags the center of her ass along my cock and fuck if I don't start to harden.

It's wrong. Disturbing.

Sure, I want Allegra with the same intensity I always do. But now isn't the moment for my debased desires. Right now, I want to comfort her more than anything. I want to prove to her that I care, as much as I'm capable of. That my feelings for her are real and true, even if they're not enough. That I know I'll always fall short, but right now, I'm here.

And I'll give her every single ounce of compassion and concern that I can.

Until I can't.

Allegra's hair tickles the base of my throat. I rub my chin along the back of her head, holding her close.

Outside, the skies open and rain pours down. Torrential. I gaze out the window, watching the heavy grayness expand. It's impossible to see the other side of the street clearly. Instead, the trees and the brick houses are distorted blobs of shifting colors and shadows.

I close my eyes and drag a full breath into my lungs.

It's peaceful, lying like this, with Allegra in my arms, and the sound of the rain falling outside.

Allegra's breathing evens out. I drag my fingertips across her stomach, gentle and soothing.

She places her hand on top of mine, trapping my fingers against her thin T-shirt. I don't know how long we lay in silence. It could be minutes. Maybe hours.

I'm heading to London tomorrow to start our European tour.

There are a hundred things I need to do. Need to consider and decide.

Right now, none of them matter.

I listen to Allegra's breathing. I savor the feel of her skin, her heat, against mine. I don't think; I dream. I don't plan; I hope.

I'm supposed to be comforting her and instead, she's giving me the greatest gift. Her acceptance. Her forgiveness. Her presence.

It wraps around me, warm and thick and genuine, and I revel in it. A moment of peace, a stretch of solitude.

Our connection is as intense as ever, even without words. Allegra and I can communicate through looks and touches. Through breathing alone.

She turns, shifting to roll onto her back before facing me. The fronts of our knees bang and my hand hooks around her lower back, my fingertips brushing the waistband of her shorts.

She tips her face up, her nose dragging along the underside of my chin, until she meets my eyes.

"I loved him," she murmurs.

"He was easy to love."

"I've never lost someone before." A confession.

"It never gets easier." A fact.

"I mean, not like this. I've lost people in other ways."

I glance at her, wonder if she's talking about me. Or Levi? Or her parents? Maybe Cynthia and her childhood community?

"Allegra," I whisper, my lips nearly lined up with hers. "I'm so fucking sorry, beautiful."

"So am I," she admits. She rolls her lips together, purses them. They're so close, I can feel their phantom touch against mine. The slightest movement and our mouths would touch, our lips seeking, our tongues searching. "I'm still coming on tour."

My chest tightens at her admission. My stomach clenches. My fingertips flex. "Are you sure?"

She nods, her eyes dark. "I need to fix things with Levi. I need...I need to have family. To belong."

"You do," I argue.

"Not the way I want. I don't expect anything from you." She gives me the out that breaks my heart.

"What if I want you to?" I murmur the question, even though I shouldn't. I fucking know better.

And yet, it's the truth. I want her to have expectations of me.

Deep down, I want her to want me to be enough. To step up and man up.

And fuck, that's a terrible thing to desire. An awful wish because I can't live up to it. All I'll do is cause her unnecessary pain.

"Do you?"

"Sometimes."

She almost smiles. "That's not enough."

"Will I ever be enough?"

"You could be." She watches me carefully.

My mind unravels at the possibility before me. At what she's offering—a real chance. The future of my dreams.

"Allegra." It's guttural, raw. A plea and a warning.

"I want you to be," she admits.

"Fuck, baby." I screw my eyes shut. I can't fuck over Levi, the band. But I can't walk away from Allegra. Not like this. Not now.

She closes the space between us. She moves her mouth over mine and I open for her, needing her touch, needing her connection, more than oxygen.

Her fingertips press against the sides of my jaw. My hand that is trapped between our bodies slides under her shoulders, tangles in her hair.

I position her head to deepen our kiss and she tosses one leg over my bent knees, bringing us closer.

I kiss her slowly. Deeply. Reverently.

Her tongue traces the seam of my lips. My fingers brush along her back, through her hair. It's lazy and luscious. Relaxed and restorative.

She pulls back slightly, drinks in my expression.

"What are you doing?" I whisper, running one finger down her spine.

"Remembering," she murmurs before kissing me again.

This time, there's more heat behind her kiss and I fist her hair and grind myself against her.

I'm already hard and wanting. She moans and I know she feels it. The heat, the intensity, the natural chemistry we've always shared.

"Allegra, Stellina, we've gotta slow down." If we keep going like this, we'll cross every line and damn us both to hell.

"I don't want to," she admits. She grabs my arm and takes the hand that's behind her back. Repositioning it, she places my palm directly on her breast. Her nipple is peaked, cutting through her bra and shirt. "Please, Derek."

I groan at the sound of my name on her lips. In that tone.

"Please," she repeats. "I need this with you. I want it."

"I'm not the guy for you," I remind her.

"But you could be."

"In another life." I want to punch myself for turning her down. Mainly because my body is going to mutiny and do its own thing if she says my name again. But also because I don't want to hurt her any more than I have to. And I'm already going to destroy us.

"In this one," her voice is steady.

My resolve slips.

She arches into me. Rocks her hips forward.

"Fuck, Stellina," I swear again.

"Please, Derek. Don't make me beg." At her tearstained face and sweet, desperate voice, I give in.

How can I not?

On a muttered curse, I seek salvation. I kiss Allegra Rousell like she's mine to claim. Mine to hold. Mine to love.

I kiss her passionately. Desperately. Thoroughly.

Our mouths move, our tongues dance, and our hands roam.

I don't know how long we kiss but when I drag her shirt over her head and discard it, the shadows on the walls have shifted. The grey sky has darkened. And the relentless rain has accumulated, rushing along the windowpanes, collecting in the gutters.

I wrap Allegra and I tighter in my comforter, creating a cocoon that is cut off from the outside world.

Here, now, we're alone. We can exist in the hope that swells in my chest. In this moment, I belong to her, and she belongs to me.

"The things I feel for you, Allegra Rousell... fuck, you are everything," I admit on a hoarse whisper.

Her eyes widen, surprise flaring in their depths.

"I don't know how the fuck to show it. Or what the hell to do with it. But no matter what happens, just know that the way I feel for you, it's real." My fingers curl in her hair, my nails catching on the dark strands. "It may not be the right kind of love, but it's love. It's fucking something."

She tips her head up in response and I capture her lips again.

Our kiss turns heated, our touches desperate. And I know I'm going to devastate us. Maybe blow up the band. Ruin my friendship with Levi.

How can I not?

TWENTY-FIVE
ALLEGRA

Derek's hands are hot on my body. His words imprint on my mind, the heartfelt sincerity behind them ripping through my soul. His kiss seals my fate, making every heartache up to this point worth it.

Each disappointment. Every doubt. All the moments of wondering and searching and hurting morph into an exhilarating satisfaction as my body, my heart and soul and mind, succumb to his.

"Allegra." His voice is tortured.

I arch underneath him, pressing my chest into his. "I love you, Derek," I admit, giving him the words. Giving him every part of me. "I always have."

He rears back and his eyes latch onto mine. Two dark pits of coal shine with gratitude. Fathomless.

"Stellina. My everything," he repeats. Then his kiss consumes me.

I wrap my legs around his hips as he presses against me. His hard length teases me, offering the briefest glimpse, a hint of sensations, of what's to come. Derek makes quick work of my shorts. He loses his T-shirt and I tug playfully on the waistband of his joggers.

He tilts his head. "You sure about this?"

"I'm sure," I confirm. I've never been more certain about anything in my life.

I belong to Derek. He belongs to me. We're an us.

An us who is desperately in love. Recklessly so.

I've known it since the moment he kissed me years ago. I felt the pull on the bus ride from LA. I may have doubted it, tried to deny it, fought against it, but it's always been there.

In some way, Derek has always belonged to me. And I've always yearned for him.

"Stellina, you are the most gorgeous woman I've ever seen," he murmurs. His eyes scan my body slowly, drinking me in like a cognac to be savored. His eyes heat and his nostrils flare.

I squirm under the intensity of his gaze, feeling more vulnerable than ever before. I've never told a man I love them. I've never felt this emotionally connected to a man in my life. My heart sings for him and yet, his look is primal.

Predatory and hungry and insatiable.

Want pools between my thighs and my heart rate jumps.

A spray of nerves runs through my limbs and my hands move to cover myself.

Derek shakes his head, his eyes flashing. "Don't hide yourself from me, Allegra."

"I," I stammer. "I've never had a man look at me the way you do."

His eyes glint and a muscle tics in his jaw. "That's because you've been with boys. And I don't want to fucking hear about them."

I roll my lips together to keep from smiling. "Jealous?" I taunt.

"Always," he growls.

Derek's body shadows mine and our mouths part at the same time.

We come together like music. A perfect harmony, blending his dark with my light. Layering his rhythm with mine. Our tempo increases as Derek kisses a path down the column of my neck. His tongue darts out, licks at my clavicle, before peppering open-mouthed kisses along the swells of my breasts.

I unclasp my bra and maneuver it off my frame, freeing my breasts for Derek's attention.

He gives it readily, touching and kissing. He savors my breasts the way he does for each part of my body. Thoroughly, deeply, passionately.

When he sucks my right breast into his mouth, his hand parts my thighs and his fingers push the lace of my thong aside. Two fingers drag a lazy line through my folds, and I groan.

He sucks harder in response.

I'm wet and wanting for him. This moment has been years in the making, a culmination of too many failed attempts. This time, we're moving in sync.

Mentally vulnerable, emotionally honest, physically insatiable.

He slides two fingers inside, and I reach for him. I roll his boxer briefs down his hips, until his cock springs free. Wrapping my hand around his thick shaft, I pump slowly.

"Fuck," Derek moans, letting my breast go with an audible pop.

His eyes hold mine. We stare at each other, unwilling to blink, as our hands continue their ministrations. The sound of my arousal dances in the air. Derek's eyelids grow hooded, heat flaring around his irises.

I drag my thumb along the head of his cock, loving that he shudders. It's a powerful feeling, having this effect on him.

He slips his fingers over my clit, rubbing slow and steady. I moan, moving my hand faster along his shaft as my eyes close.

"Look at me," Derek demands.

I work a swallow and drag my eyes open.

His gaze is nearly my undoing. He's staring at me like he can see all the way to my soul. Know that it harbors so much love for him.

I begin to grind against his fingers, sensations building deep in my core.

"That's it, baby," Derek encourages.

My hand works him quickly, a desperate motion that is more aligned with my own wants than his needs. But he doesn't care. He doesn't drag his gaze from my mine.

Derek's fingers slip inside me again. The pressure on my clit is relentless.

"Derek," I cry out.

"Come for me, love. Wanna see you shatter," he says. He curls two fingers deep inside my core and my hips lift, my pussy grinding against his palm, as I cry out.

I come hard and fast. A rush of sensation flowing through me like a waterfall. My body shakes, my mind soars, and everything feels right.

Like a homecoming. A gift. A premonition of what the future holds.

My chest heaves as my body relaxes, my mind coming down from the most beautiful free fall.

My hand is still gripping Derek's cock. It twitches

against my palm, the head weeping for the same relief I just experienced.

I squeeze him tightly, my eyes holding his.

"You're fucking perfect. My little star," Derek murmurs, his voice guttural.

"Derek," I whimper.

"You ready for me, Stellina?"

I nod. "Been ready for a long time."

He grins and leans over to grab a condom from the bedside drawer.

I release him and he rolls it on, positioning himself at my entrance.

"You sure, baby?" he asks, again.

It surprises me how nervous he looks. How careful he's being.

I study his face, trying to understand what's holding him back. What would give him pause in a moment this wonderful?

"Ready," I swear.

His hand brushes over my ribs, holds on to my side, as he presses a deep kiss to my lips and slowly enters me.

I quiver as his body plays mine like a song. He holds steady for a whole note before bottoming out and my overly sensitive flesh ripples with pleasure.

Derek breaks our kiss to capture my gaze, our noses nearly brushing. "You okay?"

"I'm perfect," I say as he stills. The slight burn eases and my body naturally accommodates him. A perfect fit. His cock twitches once inside me and I grin. "You're amazing."

He smiles and his expression transforms. For a blink, he looks truly happy, lighter and brighter and beaming. My heart soars and I commit this moment to memory.

"Don't feed my ego," he warns playfully. God, I love this side of him.

"You're mine," I remind him, draping my arms over his shoulders and clasping my hands behind his neck. "I'll do whatever I want."

Something flashes across his face. Alarm or desperation, but it's gone before I can read it.

My eyebrows pull together, a silent question.

Derek begins to move, and all my questions float away.

As he slides in and out, the only thing that matters is us. This moment. Together.

Derek brings me to the precipice twice as his body works mine over in the most delicious and satisfying way. A slow burn with bursts of need. Our hands track each other's backs. Our mouths taste each other's skin. Our bodies move in perfect sync, creating friction and desire, giving in to pleasure and heat.

The next time Derek brings me to the peak, he's panting fast. His eyes are wild, his biceps shaking.

"Give it to me, Allegra. Give me everything," he demands.

"Derek," I groan, feeling myself slip over the edge.

"Fucking love this with you," he nearly cries, his hand in my hair. He tugs once and I let go.

I break for him again, a total combustion of feelings and sensations. My body quakes, my mind reels, and my heart sings.

Derek thrusts into me three more times, hard, precise, and fast. Then, he swears my name and falls over my frame, hugging me to his chest.

We come down together, our limbs entangled, our exhales each other's inhales. Derek kisses my eyelids, the tip of my nose, the corners of my mouth. His hands brush my hair away from my face and his eyes, smooth whiskey, search mine carefully.

Rolling onto his side, he pulls me against his chest. His heavy breathing fills my ear and I melt into him, wishing I could disappear inside him. Wishing we could be like this forever.

I wrap his arms more firmly around me and smile into his bicep. I'm going on tour. We can be.

As my mind clears and my breathing regulates, the possibilities of tomorrow and beyond beckon.

Derek and me, together in Paris. Atop the Eiffel Tower. Walking leisurely along the Seine before stopping for a cafe au lait at a cute cafe.

Flying to Barcelona. Enjoying paella and sangria on a rooftop patio that gives a perfect view of La Sagrada Familia Basilica.

Rome. Lisbon. Berlin. Prague.

Kisses. Touches. Glances. Together.

Everything I've ever wanted is within grasp. Everything I've dreamed of is on the horizon.

Derek kisses my temple. "I'll be right back. Gotta clean up."

I nod, too sated to turn.

I hear him in the bathroom. Listen to the sound of the water turn on and off. The toilet flushes.

It's dark outside now. Dusk has come and blotted out the grey of the day with more darkness.

Except now, with Derek by my side, some of the hopelessness has receded. The grief and loss and longing are still there but they're not as sharp. More muted and slightly bearable.

He leans down to whisper in my ear, "I'm gonna step out for a second, baby. I need to talk to the guys."

I nod as my eyes close, the pull of sleep dragging me under.

"No matter what happens, know that this is real," Derek's voice murmurs.

The gentle whine of the door opening, the hushed voices of Maverick and Derek, a ringing phone, follows me into slumber.

At one point, I feel Derek's lips brush across my temple. "My everything," he reminds me. "Sweet dreams, Stellina." My lips curve and I sigh contentedly, sinking deeper into sleep.

I dream of macarons and spaghetti. The Mediterranean at dawn and sunsets that look like fire. Derek's beside me, his fingers laced with mine, his kiss in my hair.

The future has never looked so bright. So alluring.

Like a beautiful star.

Stellina.

I WAKE WITH A START. Derek's navy sheets twist around my torso and I smile as last night comes back to me. Then, I wince, recalling Buck's death. The heaviness of his loss, the ferocity of grief, sits on my chest like a lion.

I suck in an inhale and close my eyes against the sunlight streaming in through the window. It's much too bright, much too cheery, for the pain I feel.

Sighing, I stretch my body, loving the soreness that ripples from a night well spent in strong, capable hands.

I turn, knowing that Derek's already slipped from bed. Did he go for a workout? Or to the studio?

Wait a minute.

I sit straight up in bed, my hands groping the bedside table for my phone. Where the hell is it? What time is it?

I stumble from bed, nearly tripping in the sheets. Tugging on my shorts and T-shirt, sans undergarments, I rake my fingers through my hair and move toward the hallway.

I hope I don't run into Levi. I don't want to explain this to him until we're safely in Europe and Derek's by my side.

Pulling the bedroom door open tentatively, I peek outside. But the hall is quiet. The house is silent. I strain my ears but don't hear the boys' laughter or conversation. There is no last-minute travel bustle or the whir of the espresso machine.

I pad down the hallway, glancing into each room I pass.

"Guys," I call out. "Derek? Mav? Levi?"

No one responds.

I move down the stairs, taking them one at a time, my eyes darting over every object.

The couch cushions are neat. The butcher block in the kitchen is wiped clean. The hoodies that litter the chair by the front door, gone. In fact, the only thing out of place is my lone suitcase, lined up by the front door. Yesterday, it stood in a row of luggage pieces; today, it's all by itself.

I frown as disbelief builds in my bloodstream.

"No," I whisper, whipping around as if Mav is going to jump out and scare me.

He doesn't. No one does.

I spot my phone on the kitchen counter and pick it up. I frown when I note that my alarm was turned off. My text thread with the girls appears on the screen. Thoughtful messages wishing me a great flight and a fun adventure. There's one lone text from Mav.

Mav: See you in Europe soon, A. Message me after

Buck's funeral and I'll book you a flight.

I frown and spin around. What the hell is going on? My cheeks burn with humiliation as my disbelief grows into denial. A desperation builds in my veins as my mind tries to process the obviousness of the situation. The evidence is right here.

The knowledge of fucking *knowing* burns from the inside out.

"No fucking way."

I run through the house, tearing open doors, and screaming for someone to answer me.

My toe snags on the carpet and I pitch forward, the side of my head connecting with a doorframe.

"Shit," I swear, my hand slapping against my temple.

Pain explodes in my head, but I barely feel it. It's nothing compared to the excruciating crack in my heart. My blood drains from my face and pools in my feet. I can't move. Not forward or backward.

I remain stuck, leaning against the doorframe.

The knowledge of *knowing* sears my mind, twisting my thoughts down pathways they never wanted to travel.

The house is empty.

The boys are gone.

I drop to my knees outside of Derek's bedroom door on a wail. My hands plant on the ground, my head bowing, as I sob.

My heart breaks and my body quivers as I accept the truth.

They left me.

Derek left me.

Gone. Without a second thought.

Without a backward glance.

Without a good-bye.

TWENTY-SIX
DEREK

The plane rushes down the runway and begins to ascend into the air.

My stomach bottoms out, half from the motion of the plane and half from the knowledge that there's no way back now.

It's done. Over.

Nausea twists my intestines and my hands curl into fists.

I keep my gaze turned outside the window, watching as Boston grows smaller. Tiny. Insignificant. Until we move above the clouds and the city, and the land, the entire country disappears altogether.

Just like Allegra.

Just like me and Allegra.

"I messaged A that we'd re-book her flight after Buck's funeral," Mav comments beside me.

I nod, unwilling to meet his gaze. I'm not proud that I lied to the guys and said Allegra wanted to stay behind before turning off her alarm but, it's better this way.

Better for who? My consciousness poses the question.

I grip the armrests tighter.

"I hated leaving without saying goodbye," Levi tacks on.

"She's grieving," Jameson supplies. "Derek said she was out cold so, better to let her rest."

I nod, still not turning around. The lies I spun wrap around me like a dangerous web. It's best if I keep my mouth shut.

"Still..." Levi trails off.

"Buck's loss hit her hard," Mav offers. "She'll be out as soon as she has time to process things. Time to say goodbye."

"I guess," Levi says.

I don't say anything. I don't even look at my bandmates. Because if any of them study me closely, they'll know I lied about the whole damn thing.

But how else could I slip away to Europe without my Stellina?

And what the hell kind of a life would that be for her?

Following us, following *me*, from one city to the next. Going out every night, partying. Drugs, drinking, women. Sex. So much fucking sex.

I'd never be able to protect her. Not from my demons. Not from the animal I become when the music pounds in my temples and pours from my soul. When adrenaline rushes through my veins and the chant of my name, thousands of voices and waving hands, pulses through my nervous system.

My music is everything. It's my survival and my salvation.

She'd resent me. She'd hate me.

Hell, I'd probably make her.

Then, I'd lose the band. The guys. The only family I've got.

Probably deserve that too.

Yeah, I deserve the hell I'm living in, but Allegra doesn't.

I may have hurt her but deep down, I fucking love her.

I love her.

That's what's fucked up about loving someone.

If it's real and true, it means sacrificing everything.

Sacrificing yourself.

So I did.

THANK you so much for reading Rebellious Rockstar! Derek and Allegra's intense, emotional, and epic romance continues in book two, Resentful Rockstar.

ALSO BY GINA AZZI

The Burnt Clovers Trilogy:

Rebellious Rockstar

Resentful Rockstar

Restless Rockstar

Tennessee Thunderbolts:

Hot Shot's Mistake

Brawler's Weakness

Rookie's Regret

Playboy's Reward

Hero's Risk

Bad Boy's Downfall

Boston Hawks Hockey:

The Sweet Talker

The Risk Taker

The Faker

The Rule Maker

The Defender

The Heart Chaser

The Trailblazer

The Hustler

The Score Keeper

Second Chance Chicago Series:

Broken Lies

Twisted Truths

Saving My Soul

Healing My Heart

The Kane Brothers Series:

Rescuing Broken (Jax's Story)

Recovering Beauty (Carter's Story)

Reclaiming Brave (Denver's Story)

My Christmas Wish

(A Kane Family Christmas

+ *One Last Chance* FREE prequel)

Finding Love in Scotland Series:

My Christmas Wish

(A Kane Family Christmas

+ *One Last Chance* FREE prequel)

One Last Chance (Daisy and Finn)

This Time Around (Aaron and Everly)

One Great Love

The College Pact Series:

The Last First Game (Lila's Story)

Kiss Me Goodnight in Rome (Mia's Story)

All the While (Maura's Story)

Me + You (Emma's Story)

Standalone

Corner of Ocean and Bay

ACKNOWLEDGMENTS

As with all my books, so much support, effort, and encouragement went into this one! I've been thinking about Derek Reiner and his story since he popped up in *The Risk Taker*. Writing his journey with Allegra has been a wild ride filled with so many emotions and I am thrilled to share their romance with you!

But it never would have come to fruition without these wonderful women. Becca, Amy, Amber, Erica, and Virginia — so many thanks for your time and feedback to get this book baby into tip top shape! Your insight is invaluable — as are our many chats!

To Kate from Y'All. That Graphic. — thank you for designing covers that speak to my soul. I love the covers for this trilogy!

To Dani Sanchez and the Wildfire team — THANK YOU for all that you do for me and my books!

To Sheila and MPP — I couldn't do it without you! Thanks for the endless friendship and many laughs along the way.

A million thanks and all my gratitude to the book world community. Thank you to the romance authors for sharing lessons learned and being so generous with their time.

Thank you to the content creators for making such beautiful art and bringing my stories to life! Thank you to the readers and lovers of romance for giving one of my books a chance. It means everything to me!

And, all my love to my Home Team always.